Praise for FRANKENSTEIN M. ... SANTA

Ms. McDermott has integrated our two polar opposite images of fear and delight – Frankenstein and Santa – into a very relevant parable of redemption for a new generation of readers. As a jail chaplain and street pastor, I can say it is a Christmas story that finally delivers with hope and cheer in the depth of our winter.

~ Chris Hoke, author of *Wanted: A Spiritual Pursuit Through Jail, Among Outlaws, and Across Borders*

McDermott does something with Frankenstein Meets Santa that is truly magical. She brings two universally known characters and mythologies into one time and space to tell a story that reveals something new and important about each one. It's a remarkable accomplishment and a heck-of-a-great read.

~ Travis Mayfield, Q13 FOX News

M.J. picks up the story of *Frankenstein* where Mary Shelley left it – the Creature disappearing into the arctic wasteland of the North Pole to die. I'm happy to say it didn't end that way! Instead of finding a place to destroy himself, the tragic Creature finds the one place he was always seeking – a home. Fortunately for the Creature (and us), the North Pole happens to be the home of that ultimate symbol of friendship and caring, Santa! Only Santa Claus can redeem the Creature . . . and he does in M.J's delightful fable of acceptance and . . . well . . . love. I am sure you will enjoy this fun Holiday "twist" on a classic tale of horror. I sure did!

~ David Quicksall (playwright and director),
Adapted and directed the production of *Frankenstein; or, The Modern Prometheus,* Book-It Repertory Theatre, Seattle, WA

An intriguing story about two characters you would never have imagined could come together. I loved it!

~ Bryce Ward, Mayor of North Pole, Alaska

Frankenstein Meets Santa is a beautiful and creative story about second chances and forgiveness. While reading, I found myself thinking of Fr. Flanagan, the founder of Boys Town, and his hope for every child to be a productive and loved member of society. M.J. takes profound and difficult topics of life and grounds them in hope, compassion and sincere love.

~ Erica Cohen Moore, Director of Pastoral Care, Archdiocese of Seattle

How is it possible to combine the most classic horror story of all time with a Christmas story and have the tale resonate psychologically and morally in compelling ways? Can Frankenstein find happiness? You must read this book and share it with your family to find out.*

~ Jim Harris, Psy.D.,Clinical Psychologist, Dallas, TX

*Harris's complete commentary can be found at the end of the book.

FRANKENSTEIN MEETS Santa

By M.J. McDermott
Illustrations by Jan Harvey-Smith

Wooded Isle Press
Seattle, WA

Published in the United States of America by Wooded Isle Press.

ISBN: 0-9916623-3-4
ISBN-13: 978-0-9916623-3-3

Wooded Isle Press
2400 NW 80th Street, #272
Seattle, WA 98117
woodedislepress.com

For my husband John,
and sons Kirby & Patrick

Nothing we do, however virtuous,
can be accomplished alone;
therefore we are saved by love.
~ *Reinhold Niebuhr*

Dear Reader:

At the end of Mary Shelley's *Frankenstein*, the Creature abandons humanity and seeks "the most northern extremity of the globe" to do away with himself.

I finished the book while riding a Seattle Metrobus and was surprised that Frankenstein was headed to the North Pole to end his miserable life. I gazed out the bus window and imagined the tortured monster trudging through the Arctic wilderness, a tragic victim of a dysfunctional "childhood" that had led him to perform acts of evil.

Then it hit me – he is going to meet Santa Claus! I chuckled at the thought and got off the bus.

The thought did not leave me; I started to jot down notes about it, then the pencil (yes, pencil!) kept writing.

What follows is what happens to Frankenstein's monster after the end of Mary Shelley's masterpiece. I hope you enjoy it.

Merry Christmas!
M.J.M.

1. DISCOVERY OF AN INTRUDER

"Darn big footprints," said Gum, Chief of Elf Security.

"Yep. Darn big footprints," said F.C., Assistant Chief.

In the gloom of the Arctic December noon, Gum and F.C. needed their spiffy new LED headlamps to illuminate each enormous footprint in the trampled snow. Gum permitted himself a moment of exhilaration that made his belly tingle. Then he dutifully recorded the extraordinary discovery in his security log.

"Giant footprints," he said under his breath, though he was hardly breathing. He took another look, pulled in his upper lip, and chewed on the bottom of his well-groomed mustache. Then he said aloud as he wrote, "Barefoot. Human-like."

"Yep, human-like." F.C. stroked his neckbeard, then pointed. "Toes."

Gum aimed the beam of his headlamp at the toes of the footprint. "Not paw-like, like the Abominable Snowman."

"Or a polar bear," said F.C.

Gum nodded. "Or a polar bear."

They walked around the trodden-down area. It was just outside the perimeter wall of the village. Close enough for the owner of the big feet to observe the cottages and factory of the town, but far away enough not to alert the villagers within.

Gum examined the ancient stone wall with its carvings of smiling gingerbread people holding hands for as far as the eye could see. Centuries of ice blizzards had sanded down the carvings. In his head-lamp's beam he noticed cracks in the stonework where chunks of mortar were missing. It made some of the faces appear menacing.

"Help me up," he said, putting his foot into a crack between stones. F.C. bent over and offered his backside. Gum hoisted himself up. The wall was a little over six feet high, nearly twice as tall as he was at 3 feet, 3 inches. With his head just high enough, he was able to shine his headlamp along the top. He saw sparkling whiteness as far as the beam would go – except for the bare patch right in front of him where the rock had been scraped clean. Or maybe the ice had melted there – due to the steaming exhalation from large nostrils of a creature that was spying on the village! He shivered at the thought and F.C. lost his footing. The two of them tumbled to the crunchy snow and Gum's headlamp went skittering.

"Sorry, boss," said a flustered F.C., who helped Gum up and dusted the snow off his uniform.

"Where'd my headlamp go?" Gum looked around, trying to recover his professionalism.

"There." F.C. pointed.

Gum retrieved the headlamp and aimed it at an isolated footprint.

"Let's measure it," he said.

"Okay. Heel-toe?" asked F.C.

"Yeah, heel-toe."

F.C. jumped into the footprint. "Heel-toe, heel-toe, heel-toe, uh-huh, uh-huh . . . five." He jumped out and walked back to Gum.

"Five," said Gum, writing it down in his security log.

"Yep. Five elf-feet, heel-to-toe."

Gum snapped his log shut. "Let's see where they go."

They followed the footprints away from the wall until they faded away, erased by blowing ice pellets. They squinted in the apparent direction of the tracks. Nothing but whiteness fading into the gloom.

Gum sighed and made a decision. "Better inform Santa," he said.

"Yep," said F.C., matching Gum's sigh. "Better tell Santa."

Despite his fears and suspicions, Gum was excited. It had been four months since he had convinced Santa to create the Elf Security Agency. Like every private meeting in Santa's study, it had started with a marshmallow roast in the cozy fireplace and chit chat about factory goals with Earth's continuous population growth. Then he and Santa plopped their marshmallows into mugs of Swiss hot cocoa, sat back into cushiony recliners and took delicious sips. Gum hated to spoil the cheery spirit of the meeting, but he had to. Someone had to.

Gum coughed and said, "The world has changed." And with the straightforward seriousness that had worried his parents when he was a child ("Why can't he be jolly, like the other elf children?"), he cited data and statistics about how dangerous the world had become in the 21st Century and how it was time for the North Pole to protect itself.

"With the melting of the polar ice cap and the opening of the Northwest Passage, there are more ships and they are getting closer. A Russian submarine has planted a flag on the Arctic sea floor. And I'm sure you've heard the buzzing of a helicopter now and then. All those Arctic explorers. Plus, there are more high altitude polar flights."

"But no one has ever threatened us here at the North Pole," said Santa.

"Not yet," said Gum with a somber expression.

Santa nodded thoughtfully. He reluctantly agreed to let Gum and one other elf leave their factory work, put on professional uniforms and patrol the perimeter of the village. Gum chose F.C., his life-long friend and fellow detective story buff.

They began by studying records of past intruders to the North Pole.

Santa was right. No one had ever posed an actual threat to the North Pole. Sure, there was the occasional uninvited visitor. Once or twice a decade, an intrepid Christmas-phile braved the harsh climate and appeared at the gingerbread gates of Santa's village. These were awe-struck Santa lovers who craved a glimpse of an elf or a flying reindeer; people who wished to nab some extra Christmas without waiting for it to come along naturally. They were harmless. The drill was to alter the memory of their adventure into the recollection of a sweet dream, and gently return them to their homes.

No one had ever posed a threat to the North Pole.

No one until now.

Now there was a giant someone watching them, spying on them.

Gum's belly was really tingling as he and F.C. approached the Claus Conference Room.

"Should we interrupt them?" asked F.C.

"Got to," said Gum, raising his fist and knocking loudly on a polished knotty pine door. Without waiting to be invited in, he grabbed the wrought-iron candy-cane-shaped handle, and pulled the heavy door open.

Santa looked up with a surprised expression when Gum and F.C. marched into the room.

Gum briefly regretted his impetuousness when he saw the gathering of key Christmas players. They were seated around a gleaming U-shaped table that was lit by a U-shaped chandelier of dangling bright white icicle lights (though Gum noticed that a couple of the icicle bulbs were out). Gum recognized the Chief Elf Reindeer Keeper, Factory Manager, Communications Director, Mrs. Claus, and several others. They stared at Gum and F.C. with mouths partially open, as if they had each been interrupted during an important sentence. In that momentary silence, Gum heard a drop of water ping into a metal bucket in the corner of the room from an apparent leak in the ceiling. Then he recovered his purpose, stood at attention, and barked:

"Permission to report a security breach, Santa Sir."

"A security breach?"

"Yes sir. There's something big we have to report."

"Okay," Santa sighed, "Gum, F.C. Sit down. Have something to eat and tell us what this is all about."

Only then did Gum notice that he had interrupted a dinner meeting. He and F.C. sat at opposite ends of the U-shaped table. A wheeled food cart with mechanical arms buzzed around in the middle of the U, set their places flawlessly, and served them a savory slice of quiche with a side of rustic greens and a glass of bubbly pink lemonade. F.C. dug in.

Gum could not eat. He waited for the robot as it swung around to leave. It shuddered and came to a halt before reaching the kitchen doors, making a faint squealing sound. A flustered kitchen elf emerged through the swinging doors and pushed the robot through, muttering, "Oh dear, oh dear," under her breath.

Once the doors shut, Gum said, "Santa, there is no easy way to say this. We have . . . an intruder."

"An intruder?" asked Santa, putting down his fork. "In our village?"

"Just outside the village."

"Next to the wall," added F.C., through a stuffed mouth.

There were shocked murmurs around the table.

"What kind of intruder?" asked Serrano, the Factory Manager.

"Human, probably," said Gum. "A very large human."

"With very large feet!" added F.C., "Five elf-feet long! Heel-to-toe!"

Gum scrutinized the faces at the table as the facts set in. He was not surprised when questions were hurled at him. He sat back confidently, opened his security log, and answered them to the best of his investigative knowledge. The discussion, however, took a surprising turn.

"You know," said Ginger, the Chief Elf Reindeer Keeper, "the reindeer have been acting skittish and nervous lately. I thought they were just getting excited about Christmas coming, but maybe . . . I don't know . . . maybe they sense something strange."

"A couple of times this past week, when I went down to get the mail at the outer warehouse, I heard something out beyond the walls," said Curry, the Communications Director, with a brooding look on his face. "It was a kind of moaning or groaning or something. I thought it was the winter wind or the cracking of an ice floe, but now that I think about it, it could have been a human voice."

Mrs. Claus looked in the direction of the kitchen. "Oh dear. I wasn't going to mention it. I thought it was just young pranksters."

"What is it, Darling?" asked Santa.

"Well, you know how I leave pies and cakes on the windowsill to cool?"

"Of course," said Santa, sitting up and leaning toward her.

"Well, a couple of times over the last week or so, when I've gone to retrieve a pie . . . I've found that it's missing. Gone. I thought perhaps I was having a 'senior moment' the first time, but . . ."

"How many times has this happened, ma'am?" asked Gum, who was recording everything in the security log.

"Three. No, four times."

There was a fearful hush in the room. The only sound was the ping of another drop of water hitting the bucket in the corner. Now the intruder was not just watching them and moaning beyond the walls. Now it was possibly in their village, stealing from them. It was probably creeping up to the home of the Clauses themselves.

Gum sensed the change in the room and felt a bellyful of pride.

Santa stood up from his upholstered chair at the top of the U, and started to pace. His shiny black boots made a swishing sound as he scuffed the plush cranberry-colored carpeting. All eyes were on him. Finally, he broke the silence. "Well, Gum. F.C. It seems like you've really got something here. I'll have to address it at the Elf Assembly tomorrow night. Curry, can you help me with the speech?" The Communications Director nodded.

"In the meantime," Santa continued, "let's beef up security at the gates to the village and increase our perimeter patrols. Serrano, release six of your strongest factory elves and reassign them to security."

"But Santa, Christmas is less than three weeks away — I can't lose anyone! We're pushing double shifts as it is."

"If we don't protect ourselves, Serrano," said Santa ominously, "there may not *be* a Christmas this year."

2. THE ELF ASSEMBLY

"Just come on in and take a seat," ordered F.C. loudly.

Snow-covered elves entered through the Great Doors of the Great Hall, stomping and shaking the flakes and cold away. Parents helped their children remove their coats, mittens and scarves, whereupon the kiddos took off running and giggling, and their parents chased after them.

"What's with the uniform, F.C.?" asked an elf who was wearing yellow coveralls.

"Ooh! Shiny buttons, Fruit Cocktail!" said another factory elf.

F.C. stood sternly, ignoring the teasing. He hated when he was called by his full name (it had been his father's favorite food), but he wasn't going to show it.

A third smart-aleck elf with purple side whiskers walked in as if he owned the place, put his arm around F.C.'s shoulders and spoke out of the side of his mouth. "Hey F.C., I've been to eighty of these assemblies. What's so special about this one?"

F.C. sucked in his lips and gestured to the chairs. Then he stood silently as the normally chatty, good-natured elves filed into the Great Hall for the annual Christmas speech, as most of them had for decades. This year, however, jolly elfin chatter was replaced by cautious kidding and curious questioning.

Inside, the Gothic chamber was warm and brightly lit. Logs in giant fireplaces were burning and crackling. From the arches in the ceiling hung Advent wreaths that were ten feet in diameter – evergreen circles with glowing pinecones and four candles on each, three purple and one rose colored. On each wreath, two of the purple candles radiated with brilliant white flames. Two candles remained unlit, indicating that there were two more Sundays before Christmas. Violet, indigo and silver curling ribbons cascaded down, fluttering a bit from invisible drafts.

Outside, the wind howled in the first good terrible winter storm of the season. Ice bullets pelted the tall frosted windows. There was a whistle from cold air invading through the edges of loose window panes.

Gum and one of the new Security Elves rubbed the windows and peered out, muttering in frustration at the lack of visibility. It was impossible to see more than a few inches into the night despite the floodlights mounted to the building's exterior. A few elves wondered aloud what they were looking for. This made several other elves shift uneasily in the tiny squeaking chairs.

Santa entered without fanfare at the back of the hall and had a private conversation with Gum. One look at the red-suited leader was all an elf needed to see that this year's assembly would not be the typical spirited pep rally the elves were accustomed to.

"Let's get this show on the road!" Santa said as he rubbed his meaty hands together. All heads turned to follow him. His walk up the main aisle was greeted with cheers and, when Santa raised his arms, the elves rose to their feet as one body, visibly relieved at Santa's show of normalcy.

"Merry Christmas Season!" he greeted them. The assembly reignited their cheers. Santa gazed over the multicolored crowd and smiled in his warm, loving way. The elves finished their cheers and sat back down, relaxing a little in the glow of their leader's affection.

"Congratulations on another year of exceptional output. Earth's population continues to grow exponentially, but thanks to your skill and dedication, we manage to keep up!"

Again, the crowd rose to its feet with approving cheers. Elves nodded, patted each other on the back and shook hands.

"Let's hear from Serrano to see how far we have to go these last couple of weeks before Christmas."

Factory Manager Serrano, with his gleaming bald head and stern avocado-colored bushy eyebrows, was always well prepared with colorful graphics on overhead projections. He gave a tough but inspirational speech on productivity, emphasizing how hard the next two and a half weeks would have to be if orders were to be met.

"I know how overworked everyone is, how our workshops are crowded and our systems stretched to meet the demands of Earth's population explosion. But we're almost there and we will accomplish our goal if we keep our eyes on the Magic 8 Ball!" From behind his back, he produced a Magic 8 Ball, held it up, and asked it, "Will we be ready for Christmas this year?" He spun the ball, turned it upside-down and read, "As I see it – Yes!"

The assembly whooped and applauded with a show of dedicated agreement. Only a few elves noticed the grim look Serrano and Santa exchanged as they shook hands and Serrano sat back down.

At the back of the hall, snow was starting to stick to the windows making them almost opaque. The Security Elves gave up scanning the outdoors and turned their attention to the front of the hall.

Santa's demeanor shifted to one of fatherly concern. All eyes were on him as he took his place again at the podium.

"Normally this is the time when I tell the Christmas story and we would remind ourselves of our great purpose." He paused and locked eyes with Gum. "But, before I do that – you must be made aware of something, for your own safety, and for the safety and sanctity of our great purpose."

It was as if everyone in the Great Hall had ceased to breathe. Even the children got quiet and sat still, burrowing into their parents' embraces. The only sounds were the howling of the winds outside and the whistling through the drafty windows inside. Every elf froze in anticipation of Santa's next words.

"There is an intruder in our midst."

The elves exhaled with gasps and exclamations. Children began to whimper.

"An intruder?"

"What does he mean? What is he saying?"

"Are we in danger?"

Santa raised his arms to quiet the hall. "As far as we can discern, we are not in any immediate danger. Here is what we know . . ." and he presented the assembly with the collection of evidence on the intruder. The discovery of the footprints. The missing pies. The moaning in the distance. The disturbed reindeer.

"In conclusion, it seems that there is someone, a large someone, who thus far remains unidentified, watching us and venturing into our village to eat. So far there has been no direct threat, no hostile action. However, I have increased security and wanted to make you aware of the situation. Please be assured that keeping our village safe is our Number One priority and you are as much a part of village security as Gum and F.C. are. If anyone has any additional information or evidence to add, please let us know."

A rumble rose from the assembly as elves discussed among themselves the information they had just received.

"I know something."

"I think I *saw* something!"

"Oh my, so *that's* what it was . . . !"

Several elves stood and offered their own suspicions and

evidence to Santa. The noise level became riotous.

Gum strode rapidly to the front of the hall and leapt to the stage to join Santa at the podium. He opened his notebook, took out a pencil, and stepped up to the microphone.

"Okay. Excuse me. Okay. Hey!" The hall quieted down and Santa went to sit on his gold edged throne. "As many of you know, I am Gum, Chief of Elf Security. I'm prepared to take any and all statements anyone has on the intruder. One at a time. But I want evidence, real evidence, not just fears and suspicions."

A young couple stood and raised their hands.

"We, uh, we think we saw it," said a girl with coral-colored hair.

"Yeah. We were outside the wall . . ." said the boy who pushed long green bangs out of his teal-colored eyes.

"What were you doin' outside the wall?" another teenage elf teased. Knowing laughter chortled from the assembly.

"Never mind that," scolded Gum. "What did you see?"

"Well, out of the corner of my eye, I saw a big, monstrous shape looking over the wall, but it was a long way from us."

"As soon as it saw us, it took off running. And it seemed to disappear."

"It all happened so fast, I wasn't even sure it really happened."

Gum was writing rapidly. "Did it say anything?"

"Uh, no, like I said, it was really far away."

The girl interrupted. "What a minute! Before I even saw it, before it saw us, I think I heard it, oh, I don't know, oohing or cooing or something. While it watched, you know?"

"No it didn't," said the boy.

"Yes, yes it did. I'm sure of it."

The couple sat down, debating the situation.

"Uh huh," Gum mumbled as he wrote. "Anything else?"

The head cook at the Elf Cafeteria stood up.

"I've also had a case of a missing pie."

Many elves shivered.

"When I went to see if it had fallen off the windowsill, I think I did notice big footprints in the snow – though it was hard to tell, because it's pretty trampled there."

"Big footprints," Gum wrote in his book.

"And when I looked back up at the window, I noticed something etched in the frost."

Gum's head snapped up. "What was it?"

"Some letters. Let's see if I remember: D . . . A . . . N . . . K . . . E. Yeah, I think that's it. I don't know what it means."

"D.A.N.K.E.," Gum wrote in his book.

"DANKE," the elves repeated to themselves.

"DANKE. DANKE."

"Danke!" An excited elf leapt up. "Danke! That's the German word for 'Thank you!'"

The elves shared their surprise with one another. Another elf stood up.

Crimson-haired Candy Apple, who was assigned to reindeer exercise, said, "I think I heard it laughing. One day last week, when I was taking the reindeer out for their morning routine, Cupid and

Dasher got frisky and did a spectacular series of interlacing spirals. Before I had a chance to discipline them, I thought I heard laughter and clapping from a long way off. I thought my ears were playing tricks, but now . . ."

". . . clapping and laughing," wrote Gum.

A grandmotherly elf attempted to stand and was helped up by the elf next to her.

"I heard it too. Late at night. I'm often up, unable to sleep. It was a strange sound I didn't recognize at first because we don't often hear it in our village." Gum was scribbling furiously. "I think it was the sound of sadness. I think it was crying."

". . . crying," Gum repeated with his head in his notebook.

The elves chattered among themselves, repeating the evidence presented . . . laughing, clapping, crying, DANKE?

It was not in the nature of elves to harbor ill will or stoke suspicions. The natural inclination of an elf is to see the good, accentuate the positive and look on the bright side.

The Principal of Elf Elementary stood and seemed to speak for the entire assembly.

"Given what everyone has said, it seems like this intruder means us no harm. Perhaps it is lost and frightened and needs help. Perhaps we should try to find it and invite it in."

Affirmative murmurs filled the air.

Gum was not a typical elf possessed with a typical elf's nature. He *did* harbor feelings of ill will and stoke suspicions. It's what made him a good Security Elf.

"But, may I reiterate, this intruder has been called 'monstrous' and it is large. It has been hiding from us and should it have intentions of harming us, it very definitely *could*."

The assembly became divided and vocal. Finally, the question everyone wanted to ask was shouted out above the din.

"So, what should we *do*?"

Gum tried to quiet the agitated crowd.

Santa stood up and joined Gum at the podium. The crowd hushed and waited for their leader's guidance.

"We should sit down and listen to the Christmas story."

3. THE CHRISTMAS STORY

The elves sat down and got quiet. Gum left the stage and strode purposefully to the back of the hall. Santa nodded to his right and the Elf Chamber Orchestra grabbed their instruments and launched into "Joy to the World."

Everyone sighed and relaxed as they listened to the familiar notes. Everyone, that is, except Gum, F.C. and the other Security Elves who remained on alert, scanning the snow-covered windows for any sign of the intruder.

As the musicians finished their song, Santa thanked them and repeated, "Merry Christmas Season!"

The grateful assembly roared its approval. The Security Elves thought they heard some unnatural roaring from outside the windows too. Their muscles tightened as they struggled to hear . . . no, it was merely the savage wind.

The elves grew quiet and waited for Santa to begin.

"My fellow Christmas-makers. It is with a grateful heart that I address you this year and recite once more the story we all hold so dear. This story is the reason we dedicate our lives to making gifts and giving them at Christmas. This story is, of course, the story of the first Christmas . . ."

Santa told the Christmas story; the story of the baby born in the manger, the babe who was God's own child, born to bring peace on Earth and goodwill to all.

The glowing wreaths above the assembly seemed to get warmer, and the mighty winds outside the windows seemed to surrender some of their ferocity. A momentary stillness came over the assembly. Many elves mouthed the words of the familiar story with Santa. Even the Security Elves allowed themselves to relax a little.

Santa told of the birth, of the shepherds and the angel and, finally, the part that everyone was waiting for . . .

". . . and there were three Wise Men from the East . . ."

Elves sat up with anticipation at Santa's description of the Star and the journey of the three Wise Men to find the babe . . .

". . . and honor him with their gifts of gold, frankincense and myrrh."

The crowd was hushed as Santa described the very first gifts ever given at Christmas. Hearts throughout the hall puffed with pride in recognition of their own Christmas mission.

Then they heard it. They all heard it. Not just the Security Elves, who were jerked out of their temporary reverie, but every elf in the assembly heard it.

From outside the snow-masked windows, they heard a great long low gasp and a sigh. It wasn't the wind or the pelting of ice. It was a deep rolling human-like moan. Everyone thought the same thing. The intruder! It was out there, just beyond the windows that hid it. It was right outside, and it was listening to them.

Hearts swollen with pride were seized with terror and everyone sat completely motionless, struggling to hear the monstrous sound again, to confirm that they had actually heard what they had heard.

Meanwhile, the Security Elves became so focused that they seemed to be charged with electrical impulses. Like cats stalking their prey, they faced the windows and moved cautiously, every muscle tensed, struggling for some view, some visual confirmation of their worst fears.

Gum hissed, then signaled silently and fiercely to the other Security Elves who ran rapidly and noiselessly to meet him at the Great Doors of the Great Hall. They huddled as Gum whispered orders to them.

Santa alone appeared to have missed the sound. He paused only briefly as though for dramatic effect, took a breath and went on.

Elves turned slowly back to Santa after watching the Security Elves' stealthy maneuvers, now and then peeking back to see if the Great Doors were holding. Parents held their children in their laps and squeezed them tight. Members of the Elf High School Wrestling

Team started to stand and signal to one another that they should join the Security Elves. Gum overheard an elder elf tell her companion a little too loudly, "I'm feeling claustrophobic." He looked around the Great Hall. The only way out of the Hall was through the Great Doors, and there was a monster on the other side. "No emergency exit," he thought. "We are like mice in a trap."

Santa went on with the Christmas story and things quieted in the hall. No more sounds from outside. Had it been the wind after all? Did Santa's words calm the beast? Parents relaxed their embraces; teens sat back down.

Santa stirred up their pride again, reminding them of the meaning behind their life's work:

"As I was saying, the Wise Men brought gifts to honor the child of God. Everyone is a child of God, and for this reason, we bring gifts to the children of Earth. We choose the day of the babe's birth, Christmas, to honor the children of God, just as the three Wise Men honored the babe with those first gifts of . . ."

Santa raised his arm and all the elves joined with him and said:

". . . gold, frankincense and . . ."

Before they had chance to say "myrrh," the Great Doors of the Great Hall imploded, blasting daggers of splintered wood and bursts of ice pellets everywhere. Elves closest to the entrance dove under their seats, shielding their children. Those who dared to look up were the first to see it, and many of them fainted at the sight.

A huge and hideous man-like creature strode through the snow covered debris, walking with ominous slowness up the main aisle. It groaned. It was a mournful, dreadful sound. Hairs on the backs of elves' necks stood on end at the sound.

Santa stayed where he was, observing the monster's progress with an expression not of fear, but of concern and wonder. The Security Elves threw themselves on the monster, grabbing its legs and tattered shirttail, but the beast exhibited gargantuan strength and strength of purpose. It flung the Security Elves off one by one and continued its determined march toward the stage where Santa stood. There were screams and shouts from cowering, terrified elves. The bitter wind made the assembly shiver even more. Hats and scarves and glasses and decorations flew around the room in mini twisters. The chandelier wreaths spun and swung side to side, making the lights blink off and on again. Despite the chaos, Santa stood stoically to encounter the intruder.

When the creature reached the podium, those who were still able to watch averted their eyes at what would surely be the end of Father Christmas. The Security Elves ran toward Santa, who halted them with a raised hand. The monster stopped and gazed at him. Santa looked back unflinching.

Then the fiend opened its mouth and let go a great and ghastly howl. The more imaginative elves later swore that they saw actual demons riding its odious wail.

Having exhausted its breath in that horrible howl, the monster fell to its knees in a pitiful slump. The sound it made this time was very different. It was the sound of sobbing.

Santa stood over the convulsing giant and waited. Elves began to emerge cautiously from under chairs – curiosity overcoming terror.

Finally, the monster raised its hideous head, its sobs subsided, and it spoke to Santa.

"Here I am. You called me. I am here."

Elves gasped. The monster possessed a voice that was resonant and cultured, if a bit raspy. And, he was speaking English, not German.

Santa stepped forward, reached out a hand, and put it on the intruder's stooped shoulder.

"Who are you, sir? And why do you say that I called you?" Santa asked.

The beast looked at him with confusion. "You said my name. You called me. You know who I am. I am a gift, you said, a gift to honor the child of God."

"A gift? Help me to understand. What is your name?"

The hulking brute stood up and did something astonishing. It smiled. Through broken, brown-edged teeth it said with childlike innocence, "My name? My name is Frankenstein."

Then its great watery yellow eyes rolled up into its head and the creature collapsed into a ragged heap, its incongruous smile still caressing its cracked and bleeding lips.

4. IS THE CREATURE ALIVE?

The Security Elves rushed upon the fallen creature. They formed a perimeter of sorts, protecting their fellow elves from the beast while they prepared to cautiously investigate.

The wind continued to howl in the Great Hall and the temperature had fallen dangerously low. Families of elves grabbed their coats, hats, scarves and mittens and made their exit.

Gum shouted at his comrades to stay back as he alone approached the intruder. He poked at it and quickly jumped back, expecting it to grab or roar at him. Everyone watching flinched or shrieked, but the giant remained motionless.

"Is it dead?" someone asked.

Gum approached again and tried to turn the body over. No luck – this being was too much for one elf. He signaled for help. F.C. and three others came forward and, pushing on its shoulder and arm, they were able to lay the giant flat on its back.

The sight was startling. First of all, it probably need not be reiterated, the creature was huge. Later on, F.C. said they must have looked like the Lilliputians checking out Gulliver.

The intruder was not only huge, it was hideous. A lot of its skin was visible, its clothes being torn and shredded. Its overall color was gray, in color and texture like that of a mummy. It looked like a three-dimensional puzzle, put together with interlocking pieces, with seams on the skin. Its only clothes were shreds of a shirt and trousers. It wore no shoes; it had no hat. Long locks of ragged black hair concealed the side of its disfigured face. How it had survived in the Arctic cold was a mystery.

The question of its survival seemed preeminent and Gum examined the body, searching for signs of life.

Santa looked over the man with an expression of grave concern.

"Well, Gum," he said, "is he alive?"

Gum was pressing, with apparent displeasure, the giant's neck, in search of a pulsing artery. He held his hand there and paused, with a look of consternation. He shook his head and shouted above the wind, "Does anyone have a mirror?"

"Here, try these!" an elf shouted, handing over a pair of mirrored sunglasses.

Gum put the sunglasses to the giant's nose and mouth and everyone leaned in to see.

Yes. Yes. There was a fog forming on the lenses. The man was breathing.

Gum stood up and snapped to face Santa with the news.

"He is alive. But barely."

Santa barked out an order, "Take him to the Elf Infirmary immediately!"

Gum and F.C. gathered up a crew of the largest, strongest elves. It took twelve of them to lift the giant man and carry him through the Great Doors and out into the stormy night to the Elf Infirmary which was, fortunately, just across the street.

The Elf Infirmary had about twenty elf-sized beds lined up against the walls, ten on each side, with an aisle down the middle. Half of the beds had ailing elves in them, most of them suffering from end-of-the-toy-building-season exhaustion and stress. These elves were well enough to sit up straight when the monster was brought in and laid on the soft green carpeting between the rows of beds.

Frankenstein was very sick, near death. Mrs. Claus was a talented apothecary and concocted herbal remedies to heal him, as well as delicious nutritious stews to strengthen him. She saw to it that he was cleaned and his dried-up mummified skin rubbed with thick vanilla-scented lotion.

The North Pole's finest Elf Seamstress was called in to take measurements. After a lifetime of making elf-wear and doll clothes, Taffy seemed energized by the challenge of making clothes for a giant.

Minty, the Elf Cobbler, whistled loudly when he measured the gargantuan feet. Then he got busy fashioning size 33 quadruple E fur-lined boots.

While Mrs. Claus and the Infirmary Elves tended to Frankenstein's medical needs, and Taffy and Minty fitted him for clothes and shoes, Gum made sure they were all safe from the enormously powerful super-human who had broken through a solid wood door and flung elves aside like they were made of cookie dough. He assigned a rotating shift of two Security Elves who were in Frankenstein's room at all times. Santa had objected to these measures, but Gum had insisted. Despite appearing at ease with the monster, Mrs. Claus endorsed Gum's efforts and said she felt safer with the Security Elves in the room. Santa finally agreed. Gum had assured Santa that the Security Elves would be silent and only intrude if they perceived a threat. And it was all Gum could do to stay quiet as Mrs. Claus brushed and flossed the monster's teeth.

The other citizens of the North Pole sought out Taffy, Minty and the Security and Infirmary Elves for information on the giant. Rumors were flying around the village . . . he had a forked tongue that flicked out like a snake's, his body was hot to the touch and burned anyone who came near, he ate whole pigs in one gulp, he had to be chained down or he would destroy the village in a violent rampage!

Many of the villagers titillated and terrified one another with appalling details of the giant man's appearance and abilities. But none of their wild speculations came close to the truth of this creature's existence. His story was more horrible than the most gruesome tale any elf could invent.

When he felt well enough to sit up and speak, Frankenstein told the Clauses his story.

5. FRANKENSTEIN'S STORY

It had been seven days since his dramatic advent at the Elf Assembly. Frankenstein looked a shade less like death. He was able to sit up in his giant bed, made from ten elf beds pushed together, and he eagerly ate everything offered to him. He nodded at every kindness done for him and said, "Danke" or "Merci" or "Thank you" in a deep, gravelly voice. He seemed abundantly grateful, introverted, and multilingual. He was an enigma to the Clauses and the elves – a gracious, genteel man in an abomination of a body. They were eager to learn of his history.

"My dear Frankenstein," Santa began, "I trust that you are feeling better, thanks to my wife's expert care."

"Yes, Santa, I am much improved. Thank you, Mrs. Claus."

"You're welcome dear. And you're not out of the woods yet, you know," she said with a teasing warning tone.

Frankenstein cocked his head as though wondering what woods she was referring to.

Santa pushed forward. "Frankenstein, we are all very curious, naturally, about how you managed to come here to our village. It is not easy to find this place. How did you make your way through the Arctic wilderness? You have no team of dogs, no sled. Where do you come from? How did you get here?"

Gum and F.C. were on duty and perked up to hear what all the Security Elves had been debating since Frankenstein's arrival. How did he get here?

"Perhaps I should start at the beginning," said the giant slowly.

"Oh, yes," said Mrs. Claus enthusiastically, "Start at the beginning. Where were you born?"

Frankenstein paused, as though trying to fashion a suitable answer to her seemingly trivial question.

"I was not born, madam. I was made. In the country of Switzerland, I was made. By a madman possessed of great medical skills. His name was Victor Frankenstein. And I became known as Frankenstein's Monster."

"What do you mean, he made you? How did he make you?" Mrs. Claus asked.

31

"If you'll excuse me, madam, from the bodies of the dead he made me. He patched my body together from the parts of the deceased he exhumed from their graves. He discovered the secret of life and ignited these lifeless parts to animate a new living, breathing, sentient whole human. I am that human, if you can call me human. I am the dead brought back to life by the genius, nay, insanity, of my maker."

Mr. and Mrs. Claus found themselves leaning back slightly, as if to make a little more room between themselves and this collection of dead parts before them. Gum and F.C. shared a look and moved in a half-step. After an awkward silence, Santa leaned forward again and said, "Go on."

"Victor. Victor made me. I was his great achievement. But once I came into existence, I was of no interest to my creator. He offered no affection to me. He loathed the terrible sight of me. I was an innocent babe in the shape of a hideous monster, left to father myself. Because of my monstrous countenance, my maker abandoned me. I wandered the countryside. I hid in the woods. Somehow, I survived.

"I found myself alone and hungry for knowledge about my world and myself. Spying on a family I admired, I learned to speak. I taught myself to read. Through books I became thrilled with the story of human existence. I learned several languages by listening to humans and reading their books.

"Yet every time I sought human contact, I was reviled. I desired love and fellowship, and I was spurned. I desired companionship and acceptance, and I was met with hatred, fear, revulsion and violence.

"My innocence was eventually replaced by cruel experience and I became the thing that people believed me to be. A monster. A wretch. My heart turned to stone; my mind filled with thoughts of revenge, and I performed horrible deeds in my rage against humanity. My crimes are too terrible to describe to you good people. Suffice it to say that sitting before you is a creature who deserves the hatred heaped upon him. I have been a demon."

Gum nodded as though his suspicions had been justified and mumbled, "Uh huh." Santa shot him a warning look. Frankenstein took no notice of the exchange. He stared at his hands and went on.

"The cruelest judge is the judge within and, finally, I could bear my monstrous self no longer. Polluted by crimes and torn by the bitterest remorse, where could I find rest but in death?

"Taking no provisions, with no means of transportation, I sought the most northern extremity of the globe. Civilization gave way to tundra and eventually to the icy emptiness surrounding me."

Gum blurted out a question, "But how did you survive in the Arctic wilderness?"

Frankenstein glared at Gum with hardness in his watery eyes. "As my master knew, it is hard to kill his creation. I am not of the same nature as humans. I am more agile than they, and can subsist upon coarser diet. I bear the extremes of heat and cold with less injury to my frame. My senses are sharper – eyesight, hearing and smell. It is perhaps because my frame far exceeds theirs."

"Go on," said Santa, turning to Gum and giving him a silent "Shh!" expression.

Frankenstein returned his gaze to Santa and his expression softened.

"For I know not how long, weeks, months, maybe decades?, I traversed the Arctic wilderness. I floated on ice rafts and wandered over frozen expanse, heading ever northward. I welcomed the biting winds and blinding storms. I exulted in the agony of the frozen wasteland, hoping to be relieved of my pain by the harshness of this forbidding wilderness. I embraced this white wasteland as one embraces one's tomb. I trudged through this frozen desert prepared and hoping to die.

"When I could walk no farther, I sank to the icy ground and prepared to leave this hate-filled earth.

"It was a black Arctic night with an evil gale howling. As I lay on the frozen ground and felt the icy wind sting my face, I wept for the sad accidental person I was. My tears froze on my cheeks. My pain was colossal and I believed the end had finally mercifully come. The dark enveloped me for what I believed was the ultimate time.

"This darkness was not, however, the eternal one. After many hours or days or weeks or a century, I know not for certain, I became aware of a strange silence. I slowly regained consciousness and an eye cracked open. The blizzard was over. The sky was turning gray with the little bit of sun the Arctic steals in late fall. I was disoriented, unable to move, afraid that I had survived the horrible night.

"As I lay there with one eye open, the sky brightened slightly and my head began to clear. I was still alive! Could this vile monster die? Was I doomed to walk the Earth in eternal misery? I felt a roar move through my body and I struggled to sit up and shriek, when an inconceivable sight seized my voice and paralyzed my body.

"A small four-legged hoofed animal, a deer, jumped – nay, flew – over me, and appeared to giggle as it did so.

"My shock was complete. I had not seen another living thing in weeks or months or more. How had this little brown fellow found itself in this white wasteland? How was it able to fly? How could it be happy?

"Like a child pursuing a coveted butterfly, I became instantly enchanted and summoned my lumbering body to chase the airborne animal. It was not difficult, because the creature did not fly as a swiftly shot arrow, but rose and dove and spiraled and made the very air its playground.

"And it did, indeed, giggle. This flying fellow was having fun. The sight of it lifted my heavy heart and aching body as I stumbled after it.

"The only colors I had seen since leaving civilization were white and gray. Imagine my surprise when after several minutes' pursuit of the gifted flyer, I beheld a collection of cottages and buildings that reminded me of the Swiss villages I had left behind, with their window boxes bursting with scarlet geraniums and pretty ladies in their festive peasant dresses they called dirndls. But this vision was even more bewitching to my image-starved eyes. In the white desert before me were roofs and walkways and doors and chimneys that belonged in a sweet shop display – as though they were made of peppermint and lemon drops and meringue and cinnamon – surrounded by a stone wall that encircled the village like a rope of licorice, suspended in an endless expanse of sparkling sugar.

"Then my heart sank in a sudden realization that this was a dream, an hallucination, concocted from my addled borrowed brain. I closed my eyes and hit my head with my fists until my knuckles hurt. When I opened my eyes again, the Sweet Village still hung before me, and I was startled when a whistle hooted. Suddenly, the doors on a large building opened and out tumbled a collection of beings in colors to rival the cottages.

"I took no time to study the beings. I fell to the snow, afraid that I would be discovered by these unlikely villagers, and subsequently reviled. When I remembered the furry flyer, it was nowhere to be seen in the filtered sunlight. I did not care; I had found its unexpected destination.

"I lay on my belly in the snow with my chin in my hands, and studied the Sweet Village from a distance until the Arctic gray day gave way to Arctic night once more.

"What a different night from the one I had just spent! The previous night I had felt despair and had dreamed of death. This night I felt delight as the tiny buildings began to glitter with lamp light, and I dared to dream of another chance at life.

"There was no moon that night, and I finally felt safe enough to rise and approach the object of my new desire.

"Cautiously, I approached the stone wall that enclosed the village, bent-over at the waist, making certain I was not discovered. I reached the wall sooner than I had anticipated. The village was not as far away as I had assumed; it was, rather, tinier than I had expected. The wall came up to my chest and I found I could rest my elbows atop it. I stayed like that and studied the Sweet Village for a long while, my yearning to enter it growing and burning. Finally, I carefully climbed the wall and approached the tallest building, which was at the edge of the village.

"I could easily touch the second story of the building with my outstretched hand. I heard small sounds from within the building, like the chirping of squirrels. I wondered if this was a building for more strange animals, like the flying deer I had witnessed earlier.

"I held my breath, leaned over and carefully peeked in through a window. The most extraordinary sight greeted my wondering eyes. Tiny people in gaily-hued clothes were bustling about, putting together, painting and decorating fanciful objects that appeared to be . . . what? Tiny trains and horses and babies in beautiful dresses . . . play things. Children's play things! Toys! And the chirping I had heard? The voices of the little people as they moved and worked and conversed!

"I exhaled a sound like, 'Ooh!' and was startled to see several heads turn toward the window. I ducked and sneaked away quickly – over the wall and back into the white wilderness – until I could summon the courage to dare another peek at their jovial enterprise.

"The next few weeks I found myself increasingly bold as I approached the Sweet Village again and again. I watched the small people work, sing, play and laugh.

"The people were all of slight but bulky stature, and possessed skin of different shades of beige and brown, unlike the fair-skinned Europeans I had known. And their hair was a marvel to behold – extravagant and colorful facial hair on all of the men; curls and braids and bouffant styles in every conceivable shade for the women. And they appeared to be relentlessly cheerful.

"I also observed the full-sized man and woman who dressed in red and seemed to govern the village. I stole delicious foodstuffs from open windows and greedily savored every morsel. I yearned to fly with the tiny deer. I no longer wanted to die. I wanted to live in the Sweet Village. And be loved.

"But I was afraid. I was afraid to be feared and hated again. If the villagers did not want me, I was afraid of what I might do.

"I was afraid. Until, sir, I heard you call my name."

6. FRANKENSTEIN LEARNS A TRADE

Frankenstein looked at Santa with yearning in his eyes. Santa took a breath and looked at Mrs. Claus who was wiping tears from her cheeks. He turned back to the monster, stood up and offered his hand to the hulking form. "You are welcome in our home, Sir."

Frankenstein nodded and smiled, then pulled Santa into a crushing embrace, which made Gum and F.C. tense up and prepare to act. "Thank you," he croaked, "Danke. Thank you." He released his hold on Santa. The Security Elves relaxed.

Santa readjusted his red suit and hat, and became businesslike.

"Frankly, my dear sir, I could use someone of your size and strength here. You mentioned that the bulk of my workforce is of slight stature." He jerked his head toward Gum and F.C. and chuckled. The Security Elves smirked back at him. "Plus, with the ever increasing population of the Earth, the elves have enough to do keeping up with the toy orders. Our village is centuries old and in desperate need of repair and up-grades."

"Oh, yes!" exclaimed Mrs. Claus, "I have a list a mile long of things I need done that Santa never seems to have time for."

Frankenstein clapped with delight. "Oh, give me your list, dear lady! Tell me what you need, kind sir! I yearn to serve you . . . to devote myself to improving our magnificent village . . . my beautiful, beautiful new home!"

"After my Christmas trip, in early January, you should be hale and hearty. We will begin then," Santa said, with a twinkle in his eye.

The Christmas journey, with more gifts to deliver than ever in history, was almost too much for Santa. He came down with an upper respiratory infection upon returning to the North Pole, complete with fever and body aches. Mrs. Claus, concerned that the job was becoming too much for her husband, insisted he stay bedridden until he completely recovered from his illness and his extreme fatigue. It was late January when Santa was finally able to meet with Frankenstein, who was feeling quite well and could hardly contain his enthusiasm.

Santa had a brief talk with Gum and the other Security Elves. He thanked them for their diligence, and relieved them of their Frankenstein duty, assuring them that he would be sure to call on them should he deem it necessary. Plus, he wanted to improve monitoring of the perimeter. The Security Elves exited the Infirmary, chatting enthusiastically about surveillance cameras.

Frankenstein was energized with the idea of being needed. He was delighted with the thought of repairing and building up the Sweet Village. He had no doubt that he would be the best builder the North Pole had ever had. Except that he had no idea how to fix or make anything. He had never built a birdhouse in his father's woodshop, or even learned how to properly apply paint to a wall. He had never really created anything. His short life had been mainly one of destruction. Fortunately for Frankenstein, he was now in the most creative community on Earth.

First, Santa and he did a grand tour of the infrastructure of the village and made a list of the needed repairs and upgrades, from the most pressing to the least. Mrs. Claus also made her list.

With lists in hand, Santa led Frankenstein into the Toy Factory and took him to a corner where a good-sized work table stood, complete with tools and an almost big-enough chair on wheels.

"This is your work space, Frankenstein. Let's put down our lists and have a look."

Frankenstein looked at the lists and was flooded with shame. He had no idea what to do or how to begin. He felt his palms start to sweat and his heart start to thump. His thoughts became panicky. He wanted to run, run all the way back to the Alps, and hide out in his dismal cave all alone. Instead, he was standing before the ever-loving Father Christmas in a flood-lit factory with the sounds of elves sawing and hammering and chatting and singing – knowing just what they were supposed to do, what they were born to do.

For the first time since arriving in the Sweet Village, he felt like an imposter. How unfair that he didn't belong in this place, that he was so unsuited to the task at hand. He was loath to disappoint Santa, but he suddenly resented Santa for thinking he could do this, for having faith in him. He was a monster! He did not know construction! He only knew demolition! He gripped the sides of the table and felt rage rising in his throat. He growled, lifted the table up and brought it down with a slam.

Luckily, the sturdy table held. But all the elves stopped chatting and singing and looked fearfully at Frankenstein.

Santa straightened up the lists like nothing had happened and spoke calmly, "I understand that you probably have no training in repairing elf buildings at the North Pole. So I have assigned two senior maintenance elves to train you and guide you as you take on this responsibility. Let me introduce Mike and Ike. They can build and maintain just about anything. Right, guys?"

"Righto, Santa!" said Ike, a platinum-haired elf with a chiseled jaw and perfect ivory teeth. "It's just that the jobs are getting away from us."

"And, honestly, we're a little too small and weak for some of the big jobs," said Mike, an elf with a fuzzy turquoise beard and huge biceps and quads. He looked tough enough to ski around the Arctic Circle.

Using his muscular arms like a gymnast, Mike lifted himself up, sat on the workbench, pulled his knees up, wrapped his arms around his legs, and smiled so that his cheeks made little red apples. "What am I?" he asked, "C'mon, what am I?"

Frankenstein had no idea what Mike was supposed to be and just stared with his mouth open.

"An Elf on a Shelf!" Mike laughed vigorously. "Right?!" He made the pose again.

"Don't *toy* with us, Dude," said Ike.

The elves in the factory held up the toys they were working on and hooted. Frankenstein looked around and forced a smile. Mike jumped down and he and Ike fist bumped.

Santa shook his head, then reached up, clapped Frankenstein on the shoulder blade and said, "I'm leaving you in excellent hands, Frankenstein. Good luck, gentlemen."

Frankenstein felt a flutter of dread as he watched Santa hurry away, leaving him with the jokesters of the elf world. He felt like he needed to show them that he was prepared to be a handyman and turned back to the work table where some nifty tools were laid out next to his lists. He reached for a shiny hammer with a thick black handle and felt its manly weight. He raised it over his head and brought the hammer down onto the table with a smash. He enjoyed the feeling of swinging and smashing the hammer and gave a little growl of pleasure. Once more the elves stopped working and stared at Frankenstein. Some moved to the far side of the room.

"Whoa whoa whoa, big guy!" said Mike as he grabbed Frankenstein's arm, removing the hammer that had left a round indentation in the table.

"You're really strong, Mr. Frankenstein," said Ike, "But we've got to learn to use these tools properly so we can harness that strength, and so no one gets hurt."

Frankenstein pulled away from Mike and Ike and looked toward the door where Santa had gone. He wanted to chase after him and be with him. Who were these strangers who wanted him to learn things? He stood still as he watched them produce a block of wood and a handful of nails. Ike showed Frankenstein how to hold the hammer, toward the back of the handle to give it something called "leverage." Then Mike held the block of wood while Ike took a nail, put the sharp point into the wood and held it there with his left hand. Then, using the hammer in his right hand, he hit the nail five times until the head was flush with the wood.

Frankenstein was excited to try it. It looked so effortless and useful, using the hammer to hit a nail into wood.

Ike got another nail and Frankenstein reached for it. "Hold on," said Ike, "Let me drive it in a little, get it started for you."

Frankenstein felt frustrated, but backed off as Ike hit the nail part-way into the wood. Then Ike handed the hammer to Frankenstein and moved away, indicating that it was his turn. Frankenstein gripped the hammer as he'd seen Ike do, toward the back of the handle, held onto the wood with his other hand, raised the hammer above his head, then smashed it down, catching the nail off center so that it was bent over and pushed completely into the wood on its side. The force knocked the block of wood out of the grip of Mike and Frankenstein and it went skittering to the left, barely missing Ike who jumped to avoid getting struck. In his surprise, Frankenstein let go of the hammer and it flew to the right, over the heads of a dozen elves who ducked.

"Impressive," said Ike, picking up the block with the nail buried sideways into the wood.

Mike got the hammer, apologizing to a couple of elves who were nearly hit. "Okay," he said, "good first try."

Ike brought over the block of wood, drove another nail part-way in, emphasizing how he only brought the hammer up shoulder high before hitting it, and how it really didn't need all of his power to hit a teeny tiny nail into a pretty soft piece of wood.

"Let's try it again," he said as he handed the hammer to Frankenstein, exchanging a look with Mike.

Frankenstein noticed the look. He could see elves watching him cautiously as he took the hammer again. He could feel their fear of him, their resentment for his being in their perfect and splendid society. He knew he did not belong among them. He wanted to throw the hammer at them all, bash in their little sparkling eyes and retreat into the solitary wilderness where he knew who he was. The hammer did not feel comfortable in his hand. He was sure he would fail again and destroy another nail. He envisioned hitting his own hand and feeling blinding self-inflicted pain, or causing an accident that would harm one of these innocent little people. He inhaled, lifted the hammer to shoulder height, focused intently on his tiny target, and brought the hammer down with controlled speed, hitting the nail squarely on its head and driving it solidly, perfectly into the wood – the head absolutely flush with the surface in one solid whack.

Mike and Ike looked at the nail, then up at each other, then clapped and hooted.

"You did it!" shouted Ike.

Mike agreed, "You really drove that nail home!"

Frankenstein stroked the top of the nail, then looked up and lifted the hammer high into the air triumphantly. The watching worker elves stood and applauded. Something stirred in Frankenstein and he cautiously repeated a word he'd never owned, "Home."

Mike and Ike set up a few more practice nails. Frankenstein drove each nail into the wood with one blow. Each time, he quietly mumbled to himself, "Home."

"I gotta tell ya, Frank, you got skills," Ike said. "Now let's try it with you holding the nail at the start." He showed Frankenstein how to hold a nail with the left hand, and hit it with the hammer, without smashing the fingers. Filled with his newfound success, Frankenstein held a nail in his left hand, as Ike had done, between his thumb and forefinger. He lifted the hammer up in his right hand.

"Easy does it," Mike said, letting go of the block so that Frankenstein controlled it all.

Frankenstein growled at Mike, certain he could master the feat that looked so simple when Ike did it. He lifted the hammer, took aim and smashed it hard onto the nail, neglecting to get his thumb out of the way in time.

The pain was instant and intense. Frankenstein roared, chucking the hammer down onto his toe, which erupted in agony. He threw the block across the room, taking out a shelf of dinosaur models. The factory elves screamed and dived under their work tables, while Ike and Mike tried to soothe the giant beast.

"It's okay," said Ike, "No biggee!"

"Breathe, Frank, breathe," said Mike, standing between Frankenstein and the other elves with his arms up.

For a moment, the room was completely still and silent – the elves hiding, Mike and Ike frozen like statues with their arms raised, Frankenstein holding his left thumb in his right hand and standing on one foot. Then Ike smiled, chuckled a little, and said, "Hey Frank, it happens to all of us."

Frankenstein inhaled, and then let out a wail that was heard throughout the village. He spun around, holding his thumb, and limped swiftly out the door.

Once outside, he hobbled as quickly as he could to the perimeter wall. He thought about climbing over it and leaving the Sweet Village forever. But the throbbing in his thumb and foot had subsided and a heavy familiar feeling weighed him down. He sank to the ground, crouched beside the wall, and tried to make himself small.

Mike and Ike ran to him, but stayed at a safe distance.

"Hey Frank," said Mike, "Are you okay? Getting hit with a hammer hurts like the dickens!"

"How would you know?" Frankenstein sneered.

"Because I've done it many times," said Mike, and he held up his hands, pointing at various digits as he spoke, "I broke this one with a sledgehammer, nearly took this one off with a table saw, and the fingernail popped off of this one after I dropped a cinderblock on it."

"But you are such a good builder," said Frankenstein.

Mike shrugged, "Comes with the territory, Frank."

"And you," said Frankenstein, pointing at Ike. "You laughed at me."

"Ah, geez," said Ike, sagging a little, "I'm sorry. I tend to joke when I'm nervous."

Frankenstein glowered at them and blurted out his deepest fear. "I cannot do this. I am no good at building. I don't belong here. I don't belong anywhere." He got up. "I should go." He turned around and jumped to the middle of the wall in one leap.

Mike and Ike ran and grabbed his legs, shouting, "No, no, Frank! Don't leave!"

Hanging mid-wall with the elves clinging to his pant legs, Frankenstein looked down and said, "Let me go. I do not belong here. You are better off without me."

"Nope, no, not true, Frank," said Ike. "You are big, strong and a quick learner."

"Yep," said Mike. "And we *really* need help. The village is falling apart. You are a godsend."

"It'll just take some training," said Ike. "And not much – you really catch on quickly."

"Yep," said Mike, "And you've got a good eye."

"Plus," said Ike, "Santa believes in you."

Frankenstein held onto two of the words he heard, "godsend" and "Santa." He looked down and said, "You may let go. I will come down."

Mike and Ike let go and fell to the ground. Frankenstein lowered himself and then helped the guys up. They exhaled and dusted themselves off.

"Great," said Ike. "Give it some time, Frank. No one is perfect the first time."

"Yep," said Mike. "Hey, no one is ever really perfect anyway!"

They both laughed and said together, "Progress, not perfection."

"Progress, not perfection," Frankenstein repeated. He nodded and followed them back to the Toy Factory.

He shyly opened the door and moved timidly to the workbench. The chatty elves got quiet and squinted at him.

"I am sorry," he said to them, and he bowed his head.

The elves nodded and smiled and chirped, "No problem!" "Try again!" "You'll get it!" "You're really good at nailing!" And they settled into their work as if nothing had happened.

Frankenstein marveled at something he had never felt: forgiveness and acceptance. The beast had been momentarily tamed.

7. CONTRIBUTING TO THE COMMUNITY

Frankenstein did get really good at nailing. He mastered the skill and rarely hit his thumb again after that first day. It wasn't long before Mike, Ike and he began to attack the lists.

The most pressing items on the lists were the roofs of the largest buildings – the Claus Conference Center, the Great Hall and the Toy Factory. Frankenstein's size, strength and endurance, combined with his newfound nailing skill, got the jobs done faster than Mike or Ike could have imagined. They could hardly keep up with him. They'd no sooner send up a pallet of shingles that resembled delicious gumdrops, than he had them nailed in and polished. Soon the roofs of the North Pole glimmered with a fresh pastel sparkle. Plus, rooms beneath weren't leaking anymore.

Santa periodically inspected the work and he was extremely pleased. He smiled and nodded at Frankenstein like he had known all along what a great worker he'd turn out to be.

Next were other repairs to the Great Hall – repairing the damage done by Frankenstein the night he burst onto the scene, and caulking and insulating around the drafty windows.

The elves loved working with Frankenstein. They didn't need to move the ladder as much as when they did the high-up work themselves. Plus, Frankenstein really did have skill, a finesse. Ike showed Frankenstein how to measure and cut the wood for a new Great Door, then attach the hardware and hang it perfectly. While Mike and Ike were having lunch, Frankenstein took a chisel and gouge and carved a perfect portrait of Santa lovingly into the door. Mike and Ike were mystified when they saw it. Ike couldn't let the opportunity for a pun go and he said, "Well, Santa does have an open door policy!"

Frankenstein and Mike groaned.

Mike and Ike taught Frankenstein how to use a caulking gun and he made a clean bead and seal around each of the tall windows. No more whistling drafts during the Elf Assembly!

Once the big repairs were done, Frankenstein moved onto smaller ones.

Following the instructions of Ginger and Candy Apple, he straightened and sharpened the runners on Santa's sleigh and gave the entire vehicle a tune up. It had taken a beating the year before when Santa underestimated the effects of El Niño on the Pacific Northwest of the United States and made a spectacularly rough landing on a snowless cabin roof in the Cascade Mountains.

He helped Head Kitchen Elf Caramela move her enormous refrigerator and clean behind it, retrieving several small wind-up toys that had marched or rolled under it.

He even stitched up cracks in the huge ice sheet beneath the village. Frankenstein learned that, unlike the South Pole, there is no land at the North Pole, only giant expanses of ice that move and shift and crack. His surprising skill with an ice needle insured the safety of all.

At first, the elves were wary of the large, frightening stranger wielding enormous tools high above their heads. Occasionally, Gum would see Frankenstein dangling from a precarious eave and he would order the Security Elves to put orange safety cones beneath the giant roofer. But Frankenstein never did slip and fall, or drop a gumdrop shingle or a tool or a single roofing nail onto an unsuspecting elf below. Gum had to admit that the fellow was agile and nimble, a careful worker who appeared to take great pride in this labor.

Soon, all the elves became accustomed to Frankenstein's quiet, conscientious manner. They began to marvel at his abilities and comment on his grace – so unexpected in a being of such magnitude and ugliness. He reminded them of a dancer or an athlete as he swung a hammer or lifted a massive board into place or even when he pushed a broom. Some wondered if he wasn't, in fact, becoming more handsome as he performed these duties he so clearly valued.

All this time, Frankenstein was living in a store room off of the Elf Infirmary. At night, he curled up on the carpeted floor and slept soundly. But his thunderous snoring kept the ailing elves next door awake, and it frightened the babies. Plus, Mrs. Claus felt it wasn't right for him to sleep on the floor of a store room.

Frankenstein didn't know what to expect when Mike and Ike met him at his work table with large rolled up papers. Ike was smiling with all of his perfectly pearly teeth as he unrolled one of the papers and said, "This has been a dream of mine for a while."

Frankenstein furrowed his brow as he studied the drawing of a building that looked like a large golf ball. He looked at Ike and cocked his head.

"It's a geodesic dome! The latest in Arctic homebuilding! The dome structure withstands our extreme Arctic winds and temperatures."

Mike nodded and said, "And it's eco-friendly! With solar panel technology."

"It'll be the most comfortable home in our village. Better, even, than the Clauses'!"

Frankenstein marveled. "It's beautiful. And we will build it?"

"We will build it," said Mike, with a twinkle in his eye. "And you will live in it!"

"I . . . me? This is a house for *me*?" Frankenstein looked from Mike to Ike, back to Mike and back to Ike. "I have never enjoyed a real home before. My creator, Victor, never opened his home to me. And I could only spy on the domestic tranquility of others because the moment they saw me, they expelled me once more. I have been forever banished, alone and homeless." He shook his head and backed away, his long dark locks covering his lowered eyes. "I do not deserve this."

"It's not about deserving or not deserving," Ike said. "It just is. That's the way things are sometimes. You need a home of your own and we're going to build it. Together. No one 'deserves' life either, yet here we are."

"Here we are," said Frankenstein.

"It's a gift."

"Before I got here, dear sir, it was a curse."

"And now?"

"This place . . . this village is a gift. I do not feel that I deserve to have a home here, and yet here I am. Danke. Thank you for this gift."

"Don't say thanks yet! We still have to build it!"

Working with Mike and Ike, building a home of his own was the most satisfying thing Frankenstein had ever done. It was one big room under a dome tall enough for him to stand up straight. They also made a bed frame with room enough for his long legs to stretch out fully, a table, two chairs, and a kitchenette with a stove, sink and shelves for cups, plates and utensils. It reminded him of the cottage of a blind man who had befriended him so long ago. Except for the glass dome through which he could see the candy colored roofs and chimneys of his Sweet Village. Simple and no-nonsense. Beautiful in its functionality. It became his sanctuary.

When he was alone in his home at night, he could feel his chest glow with the warmth of gratitude. He would walk around and around the perimeter of his great circular room and say, "Danke. Danke. Danke." One "thank you" for each footfall.

Finally, it was time to do some long-range planning. The population of the world had more than quadrupled since Santa had begun his mission; he needed to expand accordingly.

Together, Mike, Ike, Santa and Frankenstein began work on a new, updated toy factory and a storage warehouse. They also broke ground on some new elf houses, as well as greenhouses for growing vegetables, with insulated chicken coops attached.

Also, once Frankenstein moved out of the storage room in the Elf Infirmary, the guys remodeled it into a new private medical room. Mrs. Claus used it as her office and for private appointments. It also served as a birthing room. The population of elves was exploding as well.

With each project he finished, Frankenstein received the gratitude of the Clauses and the elves. He found that there was happiness in being helpful, delight in being useful. Yet, despite the enjoyment he embraced in his new surroundings, a dark cloud occasionally hovered over him. His quiet, content and diligent new self was a delicate thing. Every now and then his formerly violent temperament threatened to resurface and shatter the serenity he had found.

Elves are generally good-natured, but it was inevitable that some villagers would find it a challenge to welcome this alarming alien into their strictly elfin population, despite his contributions to their community.

There was a vocal group of pessimistic elves who wondered aloud if the resources of the North Pole were being stretched too thin with the addition of this giant person. Once, as he approached the Toy Factory, Frankenstein heard a group of these disgruntled elves discussing their tremendous workload and the pressing needs being placed upon the citizens of the village.

"We can barely keep up with the work we have already!"

"We can't care for this gargantuan beast as well!"

"It's too much for Santa to ask."

Frankenstein bent low and slunk away silently, loathing himself again for being a burden to these good people. He ran to the perimeter wall, climbed over and sat on the outside, hugging his knees, rocking and moaning, and digging his sharp fingernails into the flesh of his upper arms until he drew blood. He looked up at the sky and bared his teeth and said with dripping sarcasm, "What am I? I'm an Elf on the Shelf!" And he laughed a demonic cackle.

Then there were the occasional taunts and threats like those he had endured in his previous existence. When someone called him "monster" or "demon," he gritted his teeth, felt the ugly burning in his wounded heart and forced himself to concentrate on the task at hand. The strength it took to quell a vengeful response sometimes resulted in a splintered board from a hammer hit with too much force, or a fist hole in an expanse of dry-wall that would need to be replaced. Afterward, Frankenstein was grateful he had not harmed a living creature.

There was the day a few teenage elves lit a firecracker behind his back. He was startled and turned savagely upon them, prepared for a fight. The teens were so astonished by this image of colossal ferocity that two of them fainted. One boy, in his nervousness, laughed and shrieked, "You *are* a monster!" This caused Frankenstein to slam his hand into a wall, crumbling a pillar and shattering a stained glass window. Then he scooped up the taunting young elf and was about to break his tiny spine when Gum and two other Security Elves came running in shouting for him to stop! Frankenstein froze and looked confused. The elf boy whimpered and Frankenstein's glare returned to his eyes. F.C. ran in pulling Santa along. Santa was able to calm Frankenstein down, while the Security Elves kept the other teens back.

Frankenstein then put the boy down gently and croaked, "Forgive me," covering his face with his hands. Santa acknowledged his remorse, but could not permit this kind of violence. The teens were made to apologize and clean up the mess. The Security Elves took Frankenstein to his home where he was isolated for a few days, under a kind of solitary confinement – the greatest punishment he could endure.

Two Security Elves were positioned outside of his door for the duration of the isolation. Only Gum was permitted in and out, bringing food and a book or two. On one entry, as Gum was putting food on his table, Frankenstein asked Gum to sit down for a minute. Gum hesitated, then moved to the chair closest to the door. He sat, trying to make himself tall and wide to fill the enormous chair. Frankenstein sat in the other chair, leaning forward, his elbows on his knees. He spoke:

"Chief Gum, I have been wanting to commend you for protecting the citizens of the village as you do. You have been correct to guard them from me. I have been a dangerous creature. While I am trying to become a better man, I do sometimes slip. You are not like the other elves. You see me for what I am. I am grateful for the job you are doing."

Gum was surprised by Frankenstein's words.

"But," Frankenstein went on, "I want you to see me for what I am trying to become. And help me when I fall out of line. Remind me of how it is to be a good man, as you are."

Gum didn't think he had blushed in his entire life until this moment. He hardly ever felt appreciated in this sugar-coated community of positive thinkers. As a protector of his society, rather than a blithe member of it, he was used to people avoiding him. But the words of praise from this individual, who was also born different, and who had borne the brunt of Gum's solemn duty, filled him with a satisfaction that was rare in his life. He coughed and nodded and answered the man, "Will do, sir, will do." Frankenstein smiled and thanked him for the food.

When he was finished with his house arrest, Frankenstein joined the taunting teens and spent a week with Lolly, the Master Elf Glasscrafter, forcing their fumbling fingers to do the delicate work of repairing the damaged stained glass.

As the months went by, Frankenstein gained more control over his anger and felt more accepted by the villagers. He was stopped frequently and engaged in conversations with the elves. They were curious about him and he was curious about them. He was invited into their homes for meals and asked to tell his strange and horrible tale again and again, which he did, stooped over and cradling tiny plates and cups. (Fortunately, most elf homes were large enough to facilitate a visit from the Clauses, so, while Frankenstein could not stand up in an elf home without hitting his head on the ceiling, he only had to crouch and stoop a bit to fit through doors. Then he would find a big-enough chair or sit on the floor.)

He was met with understanding and compassion by this group of uncommon people, this group of people who felt different and outcast themselves, when they stopped to think about it. Finally, he was encouraged to join in their elfin amusements. He played games, danced fandangos and bounced dozens of tiny elf children on his spacious knees. These littlest elves were unafraid of him and begged for "flying lessons," whereupon he would lift them high over his head and swoop them through the air with many sound effects.

Among the ever-active elves Frankenstein sometimes forgot who he was, or who he had been and where he had come from. He was less inclined toward furious flare-ups. Sometimes, though, walking back to his solitary sanctuary at the end of a demanding day, he would look into the windows of elf homes and see families – husbands and wives and busy, noisy children – cooking and eating and laughing and telling stories together. Deep inside he felt a longing for what they had. A dormant jealousy began to burn in him.

8. THE MONSTER RETURNS

Mrs. Claus noticed it first – she noticed that Frankenstein was holding himself with less of his buoyant enthusiasm, carrying instead the weight of melancholy. She did not know yet that this was not a new melancholy, but an old yearning stinging Frankenstein with a familiar pain.

It bothered her to see anyone preoccupied with sadness. Marrying a jolly man had been a good choice for her. She took it upon herself to discover what was going on.

"Frankenstein," she asked one afternoon as he fashioned some shelves for her new medical office, "is everyone treating you well these days?"

"Oh, yes, madam," he replied with a wistful smile. "I can safely say that I have never felt better treated and more at home in my life."

She paused, and then jumped right in. "You seem a bit sad lately. I was wondering if you were, perhaps, missing your old life."

Frankenstein answered abruptly, "Oh, no, madam, there is nothing about my old life that I miss!"

"And yet . . ." Mrs. Claus began, and then waited.

Frankenstein looked at her. "And yet . . ." he repeated slowly.

"Something *is* missing, isn't it?" Mrs. Claus probed gently.

Frankenstein bent his head down as if struggling with how to answer her, then said, "I need to finish these shelves." He returned to his work, his enormous back preventing any further discussion.

Mrs. Claus nodded, and decided to do her own investigation into Frankenstein's sadness. She had a good idea of what the problem was. She just needed to confirm her suspicions.

She began to follow him discreetly to observe his behavior. It did not take long for her to become convinced that her suspicions were spot on.

First she noticed him watching the elves relate to one another. He paid special attention to young elf couples as they held hands, spoke intimately with one another, danced at parties, and behaved in other romantic ways.

One morning, out of the corner of her eye, she thought she saw him watching while she and Santa exchanged an Eskimo kiss. When she turned to make sure he was there, he had disappeared from view.

Then, late one night, she spotted him at the Doll Assembly Line in the Toy Factory.

She had marched over to the factory to turn off a light that had been left on, then stopped suddenly when she recognized Frankenstein's huge form sitting on the floor. He was hunched over a collection of beautiful fashion dolls. She ducked back out into the hallway, stood breathless outside the room and heard him speaking graciously to the dolls, inviting one of them to dance with him. Then she heard him humming an Austrian waltz as he stood and began to move about the room.

Mrs. Claus dared another peek and saw the enormous hulk of a man waltzing gracefully with a smiling fashion doll who was attired in a glittery ball gown. Mrs. Claus smiled and watched from the shadows as he paused in his dance, pulled the doll into a gentle embrace and kissed the air above the doll's stylish hairdo.

His eyes were closed and his lips pursed for several seconds. Mrs. Claus thought she saw tears form at the corner of an eye. She was turning quietly to leave him in his private moment, when she saw Frankenstein's head fall back and his mouth open to emit a piercing howl.

Mrs. Claus froze and held her breath. As she watched, the sweet gentle giant she knew transformed into something monstrous and horrible to behold. His entire demeanor changed, his face seemed to take the form of a demon, and even his teeth seemed to grow fang-like as his lips curled back like a rabid dog's.

Her beloved friend became a madman, a true monster, shrieking and thrashing about. He took the magnificently coifed head of his dancing partner into his mouth and ripped it from her neck. He clamped the head between his teeth and growled as he swung it back and forth like a bear murdering its prey. Finally, he spat the head out against the wall. Then he tore her limbs from her torso with his teeth and spat them out one by one.

Mrs. Claus was momentarily paralyzed as she watched the monster's rampage. She felt a creeping fear for her own safety and slowly backed away from the terrible display. When she felt that the monster could no longer hear her, she turned and ran the rest of the way out of the factory. She did not stop running until she arrived at Santa's study.

Santa was sitting in his plush recliner with a mug of hot cocoa and was shaking his head while studying population statistics when Mrs. Claus erupted into his study, panting and unkempt. He stood up and went to her, holding her trembling body in his warm steady embrace.

"My dear, my dear, what is it?" he asked. "You look like you've seen a ghost!"

"Not a ghost . . . a monster!" Mrs. Claus choked out.

"Sit down and talk to me."

Mrs. Claus sat down and spewed out the events of her evening. She told him her suspicions about Frankenstein's sadness, how she followed him and observed his behavior, how she spied on him as he danced with the doll, and then watched him transform into a raging, violent demon, howling and tearing the doll from limb to limb.

Santa walked to his desk and pushed the red button he had never hoped to touch. Over the button were the letters ESA. Gum's surprised voice crackled through an intercom speaker.

"Uh, Elf Security Agency. Yes, Santa?"

"Gum, bring your team and meet me at the Toy Factory."

Mrs. Claus, Santa and the Security Elves cautiously entered the dark factory. The halls were silent. As they made their way to the room Mrs. Claus described, all they could hear was the clicking of their own boots on the marble floor.

When they reached the room, they found it dark and empty. After a thorough going-over with a flashlight, Gum flipped on the lights and the investigators were surprised to see the room neat and tidy, with no evidence of the dramatic and violent events Mrs. Claus described witnessing.

The Security Elves got to work examining the room for physical evidence of Frankenstein's frenzy and came up empty handed. They were about to give up when Gum reached behind some boxes and said:

"Hello. What's this?"

Everyone turned to watch as he pulled up the decapitated head of a smiling and glamorous fashion doll by her disheveled hairdo. Broken strands of tiny pearls hung in her frayed curls.

"She looks like a little Marie Antoinette," said F.C.

A shudder went through the group.

Santa addressed Gum and the Security Elves, "Find Frankenstein and bring him to me."

"And don't hurt him!" added Mrs. Claus, as the ESA turned and quick-stepped away.

9. FRANKENSTEIN MAKES A DEMAND

Santa was waiting for Frankenstein by the couch in his study when the Security Elves escorted him in. Santa indicated that Frankenstein should sit in one of the recliners. He did, then looked up at Gum, who grimaced and shook his head. Frankenstein shifted his gaze to the floor.

"That'll be all," said Santa. The Security Elves made to depart, but Gum and F.C. hesitated at the door, as if to set up as guards. Santa said again, "That'll be all."

"But Santa," said Gum, under his breath slowly while glancing at Frankenstein, "he is not himself. You can be too trusting."

Frankenstein sighed and his shoulders drooped.

Santa studied the apparently remorseful creature and said to Gum, "Please, give us our privacy."

Gum took one last look at Frankenstein's expansive back, then hit F.C. on the arm and said, "Let's go."

Mrs. Claus stood at the door with a tray of cookies and cocoa and waited for the elves to depart. As Santa sat down opposite Frankenstein on the comfy couch with brocade upholstery, she came in and placed the tray on the coffee table between them. She exchanged a look with Santa, smiled warmly at Frankenstein, backed out of the room, and silently closed the door.

Santa studied Frankenstein. The giant man looked uncomfortable in the plush recliner that was too small for him. He sat with his hands in his lap and his eyes cast upon the flames in the fireplace to his side. His face was without expression. Not happy, perhaps rueful, but certainly not displaying the demonic viciousness described by Mrs. Claus earlier in the evening.

Santa cleared his throat and began. "Well, Frankenstein, you have been with us almost a year now and, I must say, you have been a welcome addition to the North Pole."

Frankenstein looked up with relief in his eyes. "Thank you, Santa," he said, taking a mug of cocoa and sipping it. "A year ago I wanted to die. Now, more than ever, I want to live. Here, with you."

Santa thought he saw fear and perhaps shame in the man's eyes as he peered at his host over his large mug of cocoa.

"Frankenstein, if you were five years old, this is when I would take you on my lap and say, 'You've been a good boy this year!'"

Santa and Frankenstein chuckled. Then Frankenstein grew quiet and stared at the floor. Santa continued.

"With you on my lap, I would ask, 'What do you want for Christmas, little boy?'" The jolly light in Santa's eyes grew serious. He leaned forward and put a hand on Frankenstein's hunched shoulder. "Frankenstein," he said gently, "my friend, is there anything I can do for you? What is your heart's greatest desire?"

Frankenstein breathed out a slow, low moan. He put his cocoa down, reached into his pocket and took out the fashion doll's torso, still wearing its torn gown, and the doll's limbs, placing them on the coffee table next to his mug. He looked up slowly from the destroyed doll parts and stared into Santa's eyes. His gaze was intense and menacing and Santa felt the hairs on the back of his neck stand up. Frankenstein spoke:

"I want a companion. I want a family of my own. Santa, I want you to make a wife for me."

A log in the fireplace split and fell, sending up a fountain of sparks. Both men glanced at the fire. Santa was uncertain of what to say next. Frankenstein broke the silence and spoke, while the fire lit up his gray-green face with yellows and oranges.

"Many years ago, I asked this of my creator. I saw the love humans have for one another. I longed for this love, this acceptance. Yet, I knew there was no love for me among these beautiful people. One look at my hideous face caused humans to flee in terror."

Santa looked at Frankenstein's face. It had become more handsome to him in the months Frankenstein had been in the village.

But it was undeniably hideous. In fact, observing the face at this moment, Santa thought he saw it harden and change. No, Santa thought, this is a trick of the firelight! And he forced himself to ignore his suspicions and listen to his friend.

"Who could love me?" Frankenstein asked. "Only one like me. So I begged, nay, ordered my maker to perform his medical miracle once more and create a companion for me. A being to love who would love me too. A woman. I vowed that if he did this, we would remove ourselves from the human race and live our lives isolated from civilization. Isolated, but together."

Santa watched Frankenstein carefully. There was no denying it. Reliving these memories was causing the giant's face to transmogrify. Softness and gentleness were being replaced by hardness and cruelty. Even his voice was changing, as he went on with his story.

"Yet he refused. He said he would never create another evil being like myself." Frankenstein stood up and groaned. "Evil! This was the thing that sent me on my path of self-banishment and self-destruction – that led me here."

Frankenstein moved around the coffee table with urgency. He sat beside Santa on the couch and took his arm. His eyes glowed golden in the firelight and he spoke with desperate intensity.

"I have not told you this part of my story . . . when my maker told me he would not create a female for me, I grew enraged. I was determined to end my life – but not just my life – I wanted to destroy him with me." Frankenstein leaned into Santa's face. Santa could feel and smell his hot and putrid breath. "I achieved my goal. My maker is dead."

For the first time in his charmed life, Santa felt mortal fear. Frankenstein had made the complete transformation into a dreadful monster. His hand, like a claw, was squeezing the blood out of Santa's left arm. His teeth seemed sharper and more carnivorous as they formed a terrifying grimace mere millimeters from Santa's nose. His eyes, those terrible watery malevolent eyes, glowered with an evil Santa had never encountered. Here was a creature who had killed when denied his desires. Sitting here with his back against the roaring fire and the only door beyond the maniac holding him captive, Santa had no doubt that Frankenstein could kill again. And that if he told the monster he could not possibly make a woman for him, then *he* would be the beast's next victim. He silently regretted asking Gum and F.C. to leave.

"Frankenstein," Santa croaked, trying to sound casual, "My dear friend, Frankenstein. Your story is full of honesty, longing and grief." Santa coughed, and cautiously touched the hand that was crushing his arm and shoulder. "Indeed, I feel honored that you trust me enough to tell it to me." Gently, Santa removed Frankenstein's hand from his arm and placed it on the cushion between them. Patting it he said, "Tell me about this woman you want. What would she be like?"

Frankenstein looked away from Santa and his face lost some of its fierceness. Santa permitted himself a breath as he listened to the creature's desires.

71

"She will be beautiful, of course. Beautiful and gracious. Intelligent, witty and honorable. She will see me for who I am, not judge me a monster because of my grisly exterior. She will love me forever!" Frankenstein stood and howled at the ceiling. All of his monstrousness reappeared as he faced Santa and leaned over him. "Santa, give me what I want!"

The silence between the monster and the man seemed interminable as Santa struggled with what to tell this horrifying hulk. Finally, he could do nothing but tell him the truth. He stood and said, "I wish that I could do this for you, but I cannot."

The beast roared and threw its fists at the ceiling. "Why? Why can you not? You are the great giver of gifts. Give mine to me!"

Santa was relieved that the monster had not harmed him. He faced the creature, gaining courage as he spoke.

"Frankenstein, what you ask of me is an impossible task. I am not a doctor or scientist like your maker Victor. Indeed, Mrs. Claus excels in the healing arts far more than I do. I am a simple toy maker. I cannot make a woman for you."

Frankenstein growled at Santa and moved slowly toward the red-clad man. Santa backed away and felt the heat from the fire warming his posterior uncomfortably. Frankenstein's arms reached out for Santa. Santa could not take another step backward. Giant arms grabbed Santa in a crushing hug and Santa thought he felt one of his ribs pop. Then he felt something wet on his neck and, to his great surprise, he realized that the giant man was sobbing and trying to lay his enormous head on Santa's shoulder.

"Oh, what am I to do?" Frankenstein said through his tears. "I had so hoped that you, Santa, could fulfill my heart's desire. Where else can I go? I am so lonely. What else can I do?"

Santa struggled to move the two of them back to the sofa. Finally he sank to the cushions, both from relief and from the weight of the creature. He held the tortured giant as best he could and let the grief of years be expressed in the sobs and moans of his friend.

"What can I do?" choked the monster. "I am so lonely."

"I am here," Santa said, over and over. "I am here. And I am your friend."

10. FRANKENSTEIN THINKS IT ALL OVER

As Frankenstein wept on Santa's shoulder, he felt his rage dissipate. In its place, shame and regret flooded in.

"Friend?" he said to his comforter. "Do not be my friend! I will destroy you. Victor was correct! I *am* evil. I do not belong in your beautiful village. Banish me! I am a monster! Hideous to behold! Tell me to go!" Frankenstein pulled away from Santa and stumbled to the door. "I must go before I harm you or anyone else!"

"No! You are not a monster!" Santa stood up and grabbed his arm. "Look! Look at yourself in the mirror!"

Santa turned him to face the mirror over the fireplace. Frankenstein flinched from his image, then stared in disbelief. He saw his fierce Neanderthal brow relax and retract, leaving his forehead with a regal frame. His gaping mouth revealed sharp fangs that appeared to sheath themselves behind lips that softened from a snarl to a smile. His eyes made the most remarkable transformation. From a glare of pure evil, they seemed to refocus themselves into a gaze of angelic awe.

Frankenstein was overwhelmed at his own visage. Not only his physical features, but also his heart and perhaps his soul felt softer as well.

"You are not a monster," Santa repeated.

Frankenstein looked at his reflection again. He was not exactly handsome, but neither was he monstrous. He closed his eyes and breathed deeply. He did not *feel* monstrous anymore either.

"And I am not going to harm you. Or anyone else." Frankenstein was surprised at how true it felt to say those words.

"No, you are not," Santa confirmed.

Frankenstein smiled. "Until this moment, I did not know that I had a choice."

Santa nodded.

"May I stay in your village?"

Santa nodded again. "This is your home."

Frankenstein nodded back, then walked out of the room.

As Frankenstein went out into the bitter winds of the clear Arctic night, he felt grateful for the stinging chill on his skin. It made him feel alive. He felt like a newborn babe, a freshly made being, with a wide-open road before him to travel as he chose. He was not a monster, a puppet made by Victor Frankenstein. He was not bound by evil. He was a man with a will of his own.

Overhead, four reindeer were practicing night flying and he stood and admired their grace and prowess. The bright stars seemed close enough to touch and the deer appeared to be dancing among diamonds. Ginger, the Chief Elf Reindeer Keeper, with her short-cropped tangerine hair, was at the helm of the sleigh behind them. She waved at Frankenstein and shouted "Howdy!" Then she blew him a kiss and steered the reindeer back to their barn, singing, "Whoopie ti yi yo, get along little dogies!"

Frankenstein blew a kiss back at her as she drove off. He felt again his longing for a female companion. The feeling did not turn to rage. It became like an ember of coal in the center of his chest. He put his hands there and felt his heart beat.

The next day, Frankenstein returned to his duties repairing, building and generally helping out in the village. He could hardly believe it was nearly time for the Annual Elf Assembly. In the Great Hall, which he had helped to repair and renovate, he set up the stage and the rows of tiny chairs. Frankenstein smiled and hummed as he worked, privately cherishing the changes in his life since his appearance at this assembly nearly a year earlier.

Occasionally, he still felt that lonely pang that called out for a wife and a family. He allowed himself to feel the longing, but then chose to focus on all the good that had come into his life. As he reminded himself of the community he had joined, of how good it felt to be a contributing member of the Sweet Village, his ache subsided.

On a lunch break from setting up the Great Hall, he chose to sit on the perimeter wall and gaze at his village while he ate his banana bread and almond butter sandwich. The sun was struggling to impart a feeble dawn on the glowing buildings. Fragrant smoke floated from chimneys above roofs he had repaired, well-caulked windows were radiant with cheerful light, and the Elf Chamber Orchestra was practicing "Joy to the World." Frankenstein sighed with satisfaction. He stretched out his massive arms as if to embrace his beloved village and said aloud, "It is enough!" He tipped his head to the sky and saw a green curtained aurora shimmering. He addressed the Creator of it all. "If I never find a woman, a companion for myself, it will be fine. If I can stay forever in this beautiful village, I will be content. This life, my life, is complete." He jumped down from the wall and fell to his knees. "Thank you, Santa, for this gift. Thank you, God, for this gift."

It was the anniversary of Frankenstein's arrival at the North Pole. It was the night of Santa's annual Christmas speech. Frankenstein attended the Elf Assembly and heard Santa tell the Christmas story for the second time. He leaned forward with great interest when Santa got to the part about the three Wise Men, anxious to hear his name. When Santa said, "Gold, frankincense and myrrh," he winked at Frankenstein. Frankenstein gasped and felt his face get hot. It wasn't his name after all! Santa had not called him after all! Yet Santa had embraced him. Mrs. Claus had healed his body. Mike and Ike had trained him in a worthy trade. The villagers had accepted him. He had healed and learned and grown and contributed. He settled back, put his hands on his forehead and chuckled to himself, marveling at his great good fortune, basking in the glow of his accomplishments.

He had no idea how much more was about to be asked of him.

11. THE PLANNING SESSION

After the telling of the Christmas Story, Santa, the elves and Frankenstein buckled down for the final planning of the year's Christmas trip. It was less than three weeks away.

A huge map of the world was unfurled from the ceiling. It was color coded with a legend that contained corresponding numbers. These numbers were huge.

"These are the new population statistics, Santa," said Curry, the Communications Director, with a serious expression. "Up considerably from last year."

Santa stood before the map and studied it. "I can see that."

"And last year, he barely made it home before dawn," said Ginger. "The reindeer were exhausted!"

"So was Santa!" added Mrs. Claus.

Santa paced before the huge map. He stopped to cough several times and had to pull out his handkerchief embroidered with "SC" to cover his mouth. The stress of the season was taking its toll on Father Christmas. The assembly watched him with concern. He sat down, sighed and put his head in his hands. Finally, he lifted his head, rubbed his forehead, and said, "It may be impossible to get it all done in one night."

A shocked buzz rippled through the Great Hall. Santa stood back up and faced the assembly. He held his arms out for silence, and then said, "Let's hear your ideas!"

A brainstorming session began. Ideas exploded all around.

"What if we do two nights this year? Eastern Hemisphere one night, Western the next?"

"What about doing the Northern Hemisphere on Christmas, and the Southern on June 25th when it's winter there? Kinda like how they split up the Olympics?"

"We could do half the world this year, and the other half next year. Christmas every other year."

"Or we could give gifts only to the *really* good children. Up the standards a bit."

"For Heaven's sake, *all* children are good! Some behave badly due to circumstances in their upbringing, of course." Frankenstein sat up straight and nodded when he heard this. "But *all* children must get a gift!"

"Hear, hear," Frankenstein muttered under his breath, as he studied a crack in the floor.

"What about the girls this year, and the boys the next?"

Santa looked pensive as the elves shouted out suggestions. The Elf Recording Secretary dutifully kept a list of the ideas. But each idea seemed bound to disappoint at least half the world's children. And this Santa was unwilling to do.

Had Christmas become an impossible task? Was it time to issue a Notice to the World and announce a new Christmas protocol?

"What if . . ." a tiny elf voice rang out, "What if we have *two* Santas this year?"

"Two Santas?"

"How can there be two Santas?"

"Yes! We can build a second sleigh!"

"And we have our back-up team of reindeer!" shouted Ginger. "I can have them ready to lead a sleigh of their own!"

"Who can do it?"

The tallest, strongest elf stood and walked to the stage. He climbed up to the podium and stood before Santa. He came up to Santa's elbow. "I volunteer, Santa, to drive a second sleigh and deliver half the world's presents."

Santa looked down at the brave little fellow and shook his head. "I'm sorry, Jawbreaker," he said, "we all have our talents, and yours is building and restoring classic car models. No, I need someone large and strong." The Hall grew silent. "Someone agile and fast." The elves nudged each other and pointed at the enormous gray man in their midst. "Someone with great endurance and courage."

Frankenstein, who had been examining the floor's stone pattern while listening, suddenly jerked upright. He looked around the hall at the hundreds of tiny faces gazing expectantly at him. He rose to his feet and stumbled back a bit.

"No! No! I cannot do it! Do not ask me to leave this safe and beautiful place and enter the world again. I was hated there. Despised. And I hate *them*. Do not send me to give gifts to *them*!"

He ran through the shocked assembly and out the Great Doors into the night.

Frankenstein stumbled to the perimeter wall and looked out into the Arctic wilderness. Then he raised his eyes to the sky and wailed, "No, Santa, no! What are you asking me to do?"

The Arctic wind blasted his face and he raged against the storm.

"Do not make me leave the village. Do not make me face humanity again! I cannot go back and be kind. I cannot forgive! You cannot force me to do this!"

He stomped and roared in the icy snow.

"So, this is how it is, Santa? You refuse to do what I ask of you, yet you ask *this* of me! Delivering gifts to the children of Earth?! Where is my companion, Santa? Where are *my* children? Do you want me to do this great act of love and generosity for a world that has been nothing but cruel to me? What about *me*? Where is love and generosity for *me*?"

He turned and faced the Great Hall. There, in the brilliantly lit windows, he could see hundreds of pairs of green and gold and blue and purple eyes watching him. Eyes filled with hope and love. He saw the eyes of his mentors Mike and Ike, the Elf Seamstress Taffy, the cobbler Minty, Factory Manager Serrano, the reindeer keepers Ginger and Candy Apple, and the ever-watchful Security Elves, Gum and F.C. Beneath the hundreds of shining eyes there were hundreds of tiny smiles – all for him.

Above the hundreds of elf heads he saw the face of Mrs. Claus, the woman who had brought him back from the dead, and had seen him at his vicious worst. Her hands were on her mouth and her eyes were glistening with tears. Then he saw Santa, who reached out his arms to him and raised his eyebrows, as if waiting for a response.

He shouted at Santa through the snow-flocked windows: "You cannot make me do this! You cannot make me do this!"

Frankenstein fell to his knees in the snow and bowed his head. "You cannot make me do this," he said softly through his tumbling tears. "But I can choose to do it."

He reentered the Great Hall, walked up the aisle and accepted Santa's embrace. The cheering of elves made the air shimmer.

12. FRANKENSTEIN PREPARES

Santa's village had never been busier. Every elf was working double shifts; finishing up the largest number of toys ever built, building and testing a new sleigh, and stepping up reindeer training so that the second team would be ready to travel the world on Christmas Eve.

With his decision made, Frankenstein threw himself wholeheartedly into the work of becoming Santa #2.

An energetic elf named Cinnamon, in elfin spandex, put Frankenstein through physical fitness training. Frankenstein exhibited enormous strength and endurance. He was also fast and surprisingly agile for so large a being. He learned to climb down and up a chimney, first without and then with a bag of toys. In consultation with Nutrition Elf Nutmeg, Frankenstein calculated how many cookies and how much milk to consume at each stop to keep up his strength, yet not be weighed down. "It's like preparing for a marathon," Nutmeg commented. Frankenstein nodded.

A bespectacled elf named Spumoni gave him intense geography and navigation lessons. The maps and globes he studied dazzled Frankenstein. There was so much to the earth beyond his native Switzerland. As Spumoni described the different countries of the world, Frankenstein tried to focus on the topography and boundaries and ignore the fact that humans lived there.

A no-nonsense elf named Walnut became Frankenstein's flight instructor. Frankenstein spent hours in the sleigh flight simulator practicing take-offs and landings on cartoon-like snow-covered roofs. Once the new sleigh was finished, and his reindeer were ready for workouts, he got to practice in the real thing, with Walnut as his co-pilot. Finally, he was permitted to fly solo. As he soared into the Arctic sky and watched the tiny village become even tinier beneath him, with complete control over his well-trained team of reindeer, he felt exhilarated and happier than he had ever felt in his life. His reindeer seemed to sense his elation and pranced with a special kick that made him hoot with delight. The reindeer glanced back at him and smiled. Frankenstein felt that he and his reindeer were becoming a team.

Mrs. Claus and Taffy fitted Frankenstein for a Santa suit of his own. He had to endure the giggles and fawning compliments of the women as they witnessed the final result. They oohed and ahhed, then Taffy gasped. Mrs. Claus moved in for a closer look at Frankenstein's face.

"Oh my heavens!" she said, "You are growing a beard!"

A most amazing transformation was taking place in the monster stitched together from the parts of dead men. He was actually growing a beard! He did not even know himself until the women stood him before a full-length mirror in his Santa suit. He leaned forward and saw that a good stubble of a beard was emerging from the formerly dead skin of his face and beginning to cover his facial scars.

Taffy and Mrs. Claus looked at his reflection over his shoulder. Taffy, ever practical, asked quite simply, "Should we bleach the beard white?"

He reached up and stroked his chin. Then he turned around and smiled at the women. "Yes. Let's bleach it white."

He looked back at himself in the ridiculous red and white costume and hat. He had never felt more like a real man.

In the evenings, he and Santa sat together in Santa's study and read thousands of letters from children. Despite his loathing of the human race, Frankenstein felt some tenderness toward the world's girls and boys. He also felt regret that he had never been a child, had never himself played with a toy. But he was too busy to wallow for long in self-pity.

On the eve of Christmas Eve, Santa handed him a packet tied with a brown ribbon and said, "Frankenstein, read these letters and tell me what we should do."

With some anxiety, Frankenstein untied the ribbon and unfolded the first letter:

Dear Santa,

It has been a hard year for me. My mom remarried and my new step-dad doesn't like me. Nothing I do is good enough for him. When I don't do what he says, he hits me, and last week he used his belt. I don't cry anymore. But I grabbed my dog Buddy and shook him and yelled at him and hit him. I am so sorry. I know I have been naughty. I don't deserve a toy. But if you could bring some blocks and Army guys for my little brother, that would be great. He is having a hard time too.

Love, Alfonso

And the second letter:

Hello Santa!

My name is Cynthia and I have been bad this year. I stole some things from a store. A lipstick and gum and some perfume. I couldn't stop myself. The kids at school tease me because of my ugly clothes and hair. They say I smell. I hate that so much. I know my mom works hard, but I wish we could buy some nice things.

I'm really sorry for being naughty and I promise to be better next year. I don't need a toy. But I would love some nice clothes. And shoes.

Thank you. I love you!!!!!!!!!!!!

Cynthia ♡

And the next:

Dear Santa:

My brother and I are sick of other kids knowing that we get a "free and reduced lunch" at school. It's embarrassing. One day some kids bullied us and we got markers and wrote bad words on the bathroom walls in the school. We got suspended. We've been naughty, we know. We're real sorry.

Your friends, Jake and Andy

And the next and the next:

My dad hates me and wishes I had never been born.

I just want a friend. One friend. Can you bring me a friend?

My mom drinks wine until she falls asleep and I have to make dinner . . .

I'm in a foster home and I share a bedroom with 3 other kids. A girl stole my favorite shirt and I kicked her. They put me in a closet. . . .

My uncle smokes dope all the time and made me try some. It made me gag and cough and he laughed and I hate him . . .

I wonder why I was born. Who could love someone like me?

My step-brother touched me in a private place and now he is always waiting for me. I hate him!

I wish someone understood. I know YOU do!

There were dozens of letters like these – from the naughty kids. Frankenstein read one after the other and felt his heart break. These children weren't "naughty." There were unloved and neglected, mistreated, stressed and confused. And they were doing the best they could under the circumstances. They weren't bad. They were hurting. They may have done bad things, but they weren't evil.

They weren't evil. They felt unwanted and alone and they had acted badly. They were reaching out to Santa for kindness, understanding and forgiveness.

Frankenstein took the letters, refolded them carefully and tied the ribbon back on them. Then he hugged the packet to his chest and looked up at Santa through tear-filled eyes.

Santa met his gaze. "Well?" he said, "What shall we do with these naughty children?"

Frankenstein held the letters to his heart and said, "These children are not naughty. If you do not want to give them toys, I will. They are like me. I understand them. Someday, hopefully, with a little kindness, they will find their goodness. Like I did."

Santa broke out into a great big grin and took hold of Frankenstein's arms. "Now you know. Now you know how it is to be Santa. You are ready."

It was Christmas Eve and Frankenstein walked with Santa to the Map Room as Santa gave him a few last-minute instructions.

"Avoid being seen. Our job is to get in and out without detection. Under no circumstances are you to interact with any human. Do you understand?"

Frankenstein nodded and sighed with relief. It would be easier to give toys to the children of humanity if he was forbidden to make contact with them.

Since this was Frankenstein's first Christmas trip, it was decided that he would work in tandem with Santa. Side by side they would travel, splitting up the delivery work along the way – Santa taking one side of a street while Frankenstein worked the other.

They entered the Map Room.

"How does it look, Licorice?" Santa asked an elf who was studying global maps covered with lines and squiggles.

"Good skiing in the Urals!" chirped the Chief Elf Meteorologist as he stood up. "But seriously, Santa, not bad. Not bad at all. I'm watching a deepening low-pressure system in the North Atlantic, but overall conditions look favorable for a decent trip. No weather-related delays that I can forecast at this point."

"Keep an eye on things, Licorice!"

"Aye aye, Captain!" said Licorice with a salute, "Calm winds and fair seas, gentlemen." He sat back down and turned to a satellite image.

Santa gestured to an array of monitors. "We put in the Weather Center after that disastrous year that Rudolph saved. No more surprises if we can help it!" He led Frankenstein to an enormous globe.

"We begin our travels on the International Dateline, where midnight arrives first. Then we head westward, following the rotation of the earth."

Frankenstein looked at the globe and shuddered.

Santa reached up and put his hand upon Frankenstein's shoulder. "We can do this. I'm pleased to have a partner this year. And I'm amazed at how well you have prepared. Thank you for agreeing to do this. I know it was not an easy decision."

Frankenstein put his hands on the globe and imagined crushing it. Then he loosened his grip and set the huge ball spinning. Watching it he said, "Thank you for trusting me."

13. CHRISTMAS EVE

"Smile!" Mrs. Claus had posed the twin Santas in front of their loaded sleighs. She snapped her momentous photo and the flash caused the reindeer to paw the ground and snort. Frankenstein blinked and felt momentarily disoriented. He was already feeling awkward in his big red suit and bleached white stubbly beard.

Every citizen of the North Pole was on site to witness the event.

Santa got into his sleigh and stood on his seat to address the excited crowd.

"My friends, this is an historic moment! This is the first time *two* Santas will cover the Earth and deliver toys to the children of the world. We might not have been able to *do* Christmas this year were it not for this brave and hard-working fellow – who looks just like me! It will be an honor to share my flight with him!"

Santa reached out and slapped Frankenstein on the back. A startled Frankenstein stumbled forward a bit and his Santa hat flew off his head into the snow. Gum stepped forward and scooped it up, dusted off the powder and held it up to the giant.

"Here you go, Santa!" he said, winking.

The citizenry of the village erupted with hearty laughter. Frankenstein raised his hat into the air and everyone broke out into cheers. He placed his hat firmly back on his head and marveled at how amazing it all was.

Somehow Frankenstein fumbled his way into his sleigh and took up his reins. He gazed over the crowd and they became silent, as though waiting for him to say something. He stood frozen, unable to come up with anything to say that fit this astonishing moment. Finally, he could utter only one word,

"Danke."

The elves cheered again. Mrs. Claus cried. The reindeer snorted. Ginger and Candy Apple, who were holding the bridles to the two lead reindeer, stepped back and smiled. Ginger gave a thumbs-up and a huge grin to Frankenstein and he gave a thumbs-up back to her.

Santa shouted, "Giddyap!" and the tandem sleighs launched into the night sky, jingling all the way.

Frankenstein was relieved that they were finally on their way. They traveled from the Pole straight down the International Dateline – their start and finish line – and, precisely at midnight, began the work for which they had prepared.

At first, Frankenstein was concentrating so hard on his job that he could do little else. Flying, landing, handling the bag, the toys, the chimneys, and being quiet and swift about it all took his entire attention. He did not want to make a mistake. But the training and preparation had been superb. Soon, he found himself leaping into his sleigh, tossing the bag of toys with one hand, grabbing the reins with the other, and taking off effortlessly. After a few time zones, he actually felt relaxed and allowed himself to look out over the land and take in the beauty of the world and the thrill of this night. Santa and he barely spoke to one another as they worked, but at one point he glanced at his mentor and caught Santa looking at him with an expression of, what was it? . . . fatherly love. Frankenstein looked away quickly and stared down at his mittened hands, which were holding the red leather reins. "Danke," he said again, this time quietly. "I am so grateful."

After a few hours, with the entire Asian continent behind them, Santa seemed especially jolly. He pointed at his watch, grinned and gave a thumbs-up to Frankenstein. They were covering the Earth in record time. They *would* be able to do it all in one night.

Frankenstein permitted himself a moment of pride. He felt confident and right in his work. But there was another feeling. What was it? He breathed in slowly and tried to capture how he felt, like a snapshot in his mind, so that he would always remember this tremendous experience. He felt the reins in his hands, the beard on his face, the hat, the clothes, the belt, the boots. He saw the inky black sky above, twinkling with stars, and the twinkle-lit towns below. He felt the wind on his face; some ice pellets stinging his eyes. He smelled the effort of the hard-working and sincere reindeer. He allowed himself to open the thermos that Mrs. Claus had given him and take some refreshment. He tasted the sweet milky cocoa that warmed his tongue and throat.

It was a perfect moment. The feeling, he realized, was joy.

For several moments he felt suspended and absolutely connected to all time and all space. He was one with the universe. Expansive, embracing, loved and loving. And then a huge black shape loomed ahead of him. As he flew closer, it obliterated the stars from the horizon and ate more of them as it grew taller and taller.

He let out a groan of recognition. His perfect moment folded up upon itself and vanished as he beheld the jagged peaks of the huge mountain range known as the Alps. Within those mountains, he knew, lay his former home – Switzerland.

He slowed the pace of his reindeer team, but he could not avert his eyes from the place of his grievous sins. Here he was, about to deliver toys to the children of this land where he had murdered a small boy out of pure hatred. How could he have been so evil? And why was he being given this chance to live and feel joy? How could he have been so full of hate then and so full of love now?

Santa must have seen Frankenstein's hesitation and came to ride beside him.

Frankenstein looked at Santa and said, "I cannot go down there."

"You must," Santa replied.

"I have been nothing but evil to the people down there. How dare I return and be Santa Claus for them? I should be punished by them, not loved. I deserve no good place in their world."

"Perhaps. But someone has to help me deliver the gifts to this town. So let's get going. We have work to do."

Santa's team dove toward the town and Frankenstein could think of nothing else to do but to follow.

Frankenstein worked as swiftly and as stealthily as he could. He did not dare take any time to notice his former haunts, nor did he dare risk being seen and recognized. As he entered the tiny homes and delivered his gifts, he kept his eyes down and his ears on alert. It was his nose, however, that shattered his resolve. The smell of his village, that familiar sweet-strudelly, pine-smoky aroma that was home for him, let loose a torrent of emotions. As he raced from cottage to cottage, memories flooded his tortured mind – of families he had yearned to join, of the blind man who had befriended him, of a young couple he had watched through a hole in a wall and envied.

They were the sweet and gentle memories he forgot he possessed. He felt affection for these people who had been so frightened of him. These people he had hurt. He wished they could know him now. Now that he was good.

At the home of a six-year-old boy, he slowed his work and was careful with a wooden train he was delivering. He sat on the floor and assembled the train's tracks into an oval, and set the train down gently, making sure the wheels fit perfectly into the track's grooves. Then he moved the train around the track slowly, quietly saying, "Woo-woo." Then, "Isn't this fun, William?" He closed his eyes and saw the freckled face of Victor's young brother. William was the blond and beautiful six-year-old boy he had strangled in vengeful rage when he was his most monstrous. "I am sorry, William! So deeply, deeply sorry!"

He retreated from the room in a stupor and found himself on the roof of the cottage and into his sleigh with no memory of having climbed the chimney. He rose slowly with his reindeer team, higher and higher into the night sky. When he was certain he was far out of earshot of those below, he raised his face to the constellations above and permitted an anguished moan to escape his throat. Tears streamed down into his beard and he sobbed in huge waves of grief and remorse.

The sight of this gargantuan Santa standing and sobbing in his airborne sleigh would have shaken the hearts of mere mortals. But the only one watching was Santa himself and he simply waited for his partner to rejoin him at cruising altitude.

Frankenstein finally pulled up alongside Santa and nodded at his mentor.

Santa nodded back and said, "Having performed acts of great evil does not preclude you from performing acts of great love."

Santa clicked to his team and was off. Frankenstein followed in utter awe.

14. CHRISTMAS EVE CONTINUES

The two Santas finished the European mainland, the British Isles and Ireland, Scandinavia, West Africa and the Canary Islands without further incident and congratulated each other as they flew over the Atlantic at a leisurely pace.   They were actually a bit ahead of schedule and did not want to descend the chimneys of the Americas before midnight reached their shores.

South and Central America, the United States, Canada . . . the Western Hemisphere was going well.

The newest Santa was feeling a little giddy.   Over the Great Plains of the United States he made the reindeer buck and shouted, "Whoopie ti yi yo, get along little dogies!"

Santa laughed and the reindeer snorted. It was turning out to be an excellent Christmas journey.

Finally, they reached the West Coast of the United States just as clocks chimed midnight, Pacific Time. Soon, all that would be left would be Alaska and the Pacific Islands, and another Christmas would go down in the history books.

As they headed south from British Columbia, Canada, Santa and Frankenstein permitted themselves a high five. They were making their last swoop through the Continental United States, starting with the upper-left-hand corner of the Lower Forty-Eight.

First that isolated cut-off community of Point Roberts, Washington, then Blaine, Bellingham, Everett – south along the shores of Puget Sound. The next big city was Seattle – with a Christmas tree lit atop its famous Space Needle.

Santa and Frankenstein were making their descent when Frankenstein spotted an unnatural light near the shipyards. He veered off from his course and headed for the light. Santa groaned, "Oh no – where is he going?" and had to pull up quickly in order to follow him.

Nearer the light, it became apparent that a building was on fire. It was a warehouse near the waterfront. Frankenstein hovered over the flaming building as if mesmerized by the glow. Emergency sirens could be heard in the distance and Santa became anxious to leave lest he and Frankenstein be spotted by humans.

"Come on, Frankenstein. It is a warehouse fire. We are not to interfere."

Frankenstein cocked his head and said, "I think there is someone in there."

Santa struggled to hear, but all he could make out were the approaching sirens. "No, Frankenstein. We are far from where any people live. Please, let us go and continue what we came to do."

He made a move to turn around when Frankenstein clucked at his reindeer and made a rapid descent, landing on the barely intact roof of the burning warehouse.

"No!" shouted Santa, to no avail. "We may not interfere!" He could see Frankenstein's reindeer flinching and pawing from the heat beneath their hooves. Frankenstein gave them the sign to stay, and the well-trained animals froze as their master found a roof exit, forced it open and disappeared into the inferno.

Santa could only wait and hope for the best as his friend put himself in harm's way.

It felt like an eternity, but finally Frankenstein emerged from the roof exit, holding a limp bundle of something. He laid it gently in his sleigh, gave the reindeer the up command and lifted off from the building, just as the roof collapsed beneath them.

He flew to Santa who signaled to him to fly higher so that they would remain undetected by the firefighters who were beginning to arrive.

Hidden above the clouds, Frankenstein said to Santa, "It is a woman. She is very badly hurt, but alive."

Santa was flummoxed by this surprising turn of events, but his Christmas professionalism quickly took over. "Take her back to the North Pole and summon Mrs. Claus. Perhaps she can help her."

"What about Christmas?" asked Frankenstein.

"Give me your toys. We are almost done. I can finish this alone."

Frankenstein climbed into the back of his sleigh, pulled out his almost empty bag of toys and tossed it to Santa. He regained his seat and, with a snap of the reins, sped northward into the dark Christmas sky.

15. THE WOMAN

It was touch and go for the woman Frankenstein had rescued from the warehouse fire. She had inhaled a lot of smoke and was horribly burned over most of her body. Mrs. Claus and a team of Infirmary Elves labored around the clock to save her life and ease her suffering.

Frankenstein sat beside the injured creature almost constantly. He studied her heavy bandages and endured the sounds of her terrible groans. Perhaps he should have let her die, he thought. Surely it was torture for her to continue to live.

Mrs. Claus asked to speak to him in private. Out of earshot of the woman, Mrs. Claus reported on her precarious condition.

"She is very bad, Frankenstein. I believe she will live, but she is terribly burned, as you know. She will be in pain for a long time, she will need an extensive period of rehabilitation, and she will be heavily scarred." Frankenstein looked at the floor. He knew how difficult it was to be horribly scarred and considered hideous. His heart ached for the dear lady.

"But there is one more thing." Mrs. Claus put a hand on Frankenstein's arm. Then she said something that confirmed for him the rightness of his actions on Christmas Eve. "She is pregnant. About five months along." She paused. "I am not certain that the baby will survive."

From the place where Mrs. Claus touched Frankenstein, it was as though a jolt of electricity shot up his arm, around his shoulder and straight into his heart. Never had he been so overwhelmed by emotions. He sank to his knees and hugged Mrs. Claus about her shoulders, holding onto her and hoping he wouldn't keel over and take her with him.

Mrs. Claus rubbed his head as he said unintelligible things like, "Oh, oh, my dear, my dear."

He got up saying, "I must see her," and stumbled back into Mrs. Claus's private medical room where the woman lay. He fell to his knees at the side of her bed. He took her bandaged hand gently, so as not to cause her pain, and he whispered, "Live, oh please live." He was talking to the woman *and* the baby.

He felt her unconscious body give a shudder and looked at her face. She made some groaning sounds as her bald brow line frowned and flexed. It looked like she was trying to remember how to open her eyes. Frankenstein's heart beat rapidly as he watched her struggle to awake. He drew closer and closer to her, studying her laboring eyelids. Finally one lash-less and red rimmed eye opened a crack, then the other. She looked confused as she tried to focus her vision. She looked at Frankenstein and he stood up and grinned at her.

Then she screamed a raspy, hoarse scream from her smoke-damaged throat. Frankenstein was shocked, but he recognized the scream and fled from the room.

Mrs. Claus came running. "What happened?" she asked.

Bitterly, Frankenstein said, "She is awake. And she is terrified of me."

Throughout January, Frankenstein sat on a bench outside the woman's room keeping vigil. He dared a peek in every now and then, but he kept his wretched body outside the door.

Mrs. Claus reported periodically on the condition of the woman. She was improving and, occasionally, briefly conscious. The baby was holding on. Frankenstein continued to sit outside the door and wait.

Santa came by frequently to check on the woman and converse with his Christmas partner.

"Thanks to you, my man, we did Christmas in record time this year. With no decrease in quality! It was an honor to share the trip with you. I hope you will continue to ride with me in the future."

"Thank you, Santa," said Frankenstein. "It was the best night of my life." And he looked at the woman's door.

"How is she?" Santa asked gently.

"I'm not sure."

The door opened and Mrs. Claus emerged. Frankenstein stood to hear her latest words.

Mrs. Claus looked up at Frankenstein with a cocked head and a twinkle in her eye. "She wants to meet the man who saved her."

Frankenstein was paralyzed.

Mrs. Claus went on. "I explained about you as best I could, Frankenstein dear. She says she is beginning to remember things, but before she will talk, she wants to meet you."

Frankenstein's heart fluttered with dread and expectation. He did not want to scare her again. Mrs. Claus moved aside and Santa gave him a slight push.

He stepped into the familiar room and saw the bandaged figure on the white bed, staring out the window at the icy land outside. As he entered, his foot made a scraping sound and her head turned in his direction. He froze in panic as her fire-ravaged face slowly found him. When she set her eyes upon him, she gasped and began to cough and cough. Frankenstein made a move to retreat, but she put her hand out and rasped, "No! Stay!"

Mrs. Claus hurried in and gave her a drink of tonic. Frankenstein moved closer to the bed and sat in the chair beside it, so as not to tower so ominously over her.

With ice blue piercing eyes, she studied the monster of a man sitting beside her. Finally she said, "When I first woke up and saw you, I thought I had died and gone to Hell."

There was a pause and then the woman laughed. She reached out the bandaged stump at the end of her arm and Frankenstein gently held it.

The woman spoke again. "I understand you saved my life. Your name is Frankenstein and you saved my life."

"Yes," said Frankenstein.

"I don't know whether to thank you or to curse you." She pulled her arm away, shifted her weight and winced.

Frankenstein clasped his empty hands together, and then dared a question.

"What is your name?" he asked.

The woman looked over, her scarred eyelids narrowing. "It's Evelyn. But I always hated my name. As a girl I had long, beautiful golden hair." She motioned upwards with her eyes. "So I made everyone call me Goldie." She laughed a bitter laugh that triggered another coughing fit. Mrs. Claus rushed to her with the cough medicine and indicated to Frankenstein that this conversation was over.

Frankenstein left quietly, slowly mouthing the word "Goldie."

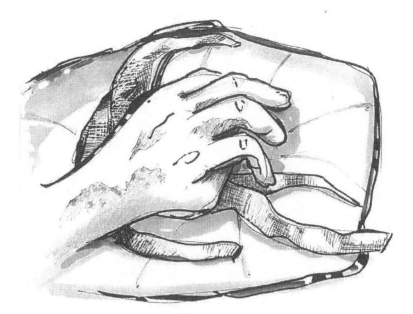

16. GOLDIE'S STORY

Mrs. Claus called her a tough cookie. She and Frankenstein never saw her cry – despite her obvious pain and frightening prognosis. Even word from Mrs. Claus that her baby was in trouble did not faze her. She simply nodded and examined the ceiling. It was impossible to tell what she was thinking or feeling behind all the bandages, so Frankenstein decided to ask.

"Goldie, what do you feel about the baby?"

Continuing to stare at the ceiling, she said with her raspy voice, "Nothing, really. Getting pregnant was the final straw. I couldn't handle a baby. I can barely handle myself. And I couldn't afford an abortion."

She paused, and then turned to look at Frankenstein and Mrs. Claus.

Suddenly Frankenstein understood it all. "You did it, didn't you? You started the fire."

"I wanted to end it all, big guy. My life has been nothing but, uh, a series of bad events. I have been a very naughty person, Santa Frankenstein. You don't know. Everyone would be better off with me gone – including this baby."

Frankenstein was about to say something, but Mrs. Claus put a hand on his shoulder and he settled back in his chair.

Mrs. Claus gently asked, "Can you tell us about yourself?"

Goldie breathed a heavy sigh. "Yeah, sure. I guess. I mean, I'm just kinda repeating history here. I never wanted to be like my mom. But just like her, I am with child and without husband and prospects do not look good.

"I mean, my mom tried to be a mom. But she just couldn't do it all alone. I never knew my dad. One day, when I was three or so, my mom took me to see her father. I remember it as a nice day – sunny, warm. They took me to a playground and put me on a swing. I was pushed first by my mother, then by my grandfather. There were lots of trees and the leaves were twisting and reflecting bits of sunlight. I remember being swung higher and higher and watching my mother watch me, and yelling, 'Look Mama! Look at me!' She smiled and waved, then she put her hands to her eyes. I remember Grandpa was singing and every time I got to the top of a swing, I put my head back and opened my mouth and gave a big 'Ahhh!' Then on a down swing, I looked for my mother again and she was gone. Just gone. Empty space where she had been."

Mrs. Claus gasped. Goldie did not seem to notice.

"I screamed, 'Stop stop stop!' and my grandpa brought the swing to a halt. I jumped off and screamed, 'Mama!' and ran to the last place I saw her. 'Mama!' I ran to a brick building with a bathroom. Empty. 'Mama, Mama!' I ran back to where my grandpa was holding one side of the motionless swing and staring at me with the saddest eyes ever. 'Mama?' I asked. He shook his head and held his arms out to me. I ran away and ran and ran. He ran after me. Eventually, I couldn't run anymore and I fell to the ground sobbing. Grandpa ran up to me and sat next to me, panting. Finally, he touched my head and said, 'It's you and me now, kiddo. Let's go home.'" She stopped talking and coughed a little. Mrs. Claus brought her a glass of water with a straw and she took a couple of sips.

When she settled back again, Frankenstein asked, "You went to live with your grandfather?"

"Yep. For the next five years, I lived with Grandpa. But I didn't make it easy on him. I was an active, stubborn child who threw tantrums. I even bit him once. But he put up with me. He did spank me, but only when I really deserved it.

"He would say things about how he didn't do a very good job of raising my mother. He hadn't been a good father or husband. I never met my grandma either. He said he wanted to be a good grandfather.

"He took me to the library and we picked out colorful books that he would read to me every night. He even got a book on cooking and taught himself to make good meals for us.

"I remember he loved to brush my long golden hair and braid it or put it into ponytails. And he always sang sweet little songs while he did it. He was the first person to call me Goldie.

"When I went to school, he made sure I did my work and went in and talked with teachers when I was bad. Then he set me straight. He was tough and quite an enforcer. But I loved him.

"He died when I was eight. They couldn't find my mom or any other family member, so they dumped me in foster care."

"Oh no," said Mrs. Claus.

"Oh no is right! That was a nightmare for me. I was sad and angry that my mother had abandoned me and my grandpa had died and I had nobody else. I had trouble behaving, especially when another kid said something mean, or a foster parent tried to tell me what to do. I did all sorts of bad things – I broke dishes, stole from a foster mom's purse, fought with my foster brothers and sisters, stuff like that. I bounced from foster home to foster home.

"The foster parents tried, I guess, but I never trusted them. Then when I got older, like twelve or thirteen, some of the older boys, and a couple of the foster dads, starting acting weird – touching my hair, then touching me in other places. You know. Sometimes more than that. It was disgusting.

"I finally ran away. Since I was fourteen I've been on the street. Seattle is pretty good for homeless youth. There are shelters and centers and soup kitchens. I mean, it's still dangerous and the rain sucks when you're on the street and stuff. Plus, there's a lot of – uh – substance abuse. And, yeah, I did some of that. It felt good to lose myself and dampen the pain and loneliness for a while.

"I met a guy, Jeffrey, who played guitar and we would jam. I learned I could sing a little. I taught him a couple of my grandpa's songs. We did some busking at the Pike Place Market, getting handouts from the tourists, and sometimes taking things from tourists. Jeffrey kept saying how we should move to L.A. and try to 'make it.' And one day he just left. Another empty space. But he left something behind."

She touched her belly. Mrs. Claus and Frankenstein exchanged a look.

"Blah, blah, blah – who hasn't heard this story? Poor little foster kid becomes a homeless teen, lives on the street, does drugs, gets a tongue stud, see?" she stuck out her tongue and showed Frankenstein the hole in it. Frankenstein nodded. Mrs. Claus bent over to see as well. Goldie shrugged and went on. "She engages in petty crime to get by, messes around, gets pregnant, hates herself and what she's become. She sees no reason to go on living and decides to end it all. One less pitiful drag on society. 'The world will be a better place without me,' she thinks as she makes her plan."

Frankenstein inhaled quietly, remembering the letters from the naughty kids. Goldie continued.

"So I picked Christmas Eve – the most disappointing night every year of my pathetic life – to do it. I had it all – an empty place, a bottle of booze and some matches. I did it too! I lit the fire. I felt and smelled my burning flesh. It felt good to hurt so much – I deserved it! I remember screaming one big scream of rage and pain. I was done with this miserable life. I honestly thought I was dead. Then you – a big giant monster Santa Claus – you come crashing in and the next thing I know, I'm at the North Pole where Mrs. Claus and the elves are taking care of me." She looked at the ceiling again and shouted: "Freak out!"

Frankenstein held his breath.

Goldie got a little quieter. "And the weirdest thing is *not* the elves or Santa or even you – but the change in me." Frankenstein leaned in and saw something form at the corner of her eye. It was a tear. "I don't know what's going on, but I feel different. Frankenstein, I'm sorry I did it. I want to live. And I do want this baby, I guess." She started to cry in earnest. "I'm going to be a horrible mother. I'm a very bad person. Frankenstein, Mrs. Claus, I've done some terrible things. But I've got this second chance, you know? And I want to take it."

Frankenstein gently touched her bandaged arm. "Reach for it, Goldie, this new life, this good life. Reach for it – for yourself, and for the baby."

"But I don't deserve it!" she protested. "How can I be a good mother, a good person, even, after all that I've done?"

Frankenstein smiled.

"Someone wise once said to me: Having performed acts of great evil does not preclude you from performing acts of great love."

Goldie gazed into Frankenstein's eyes through her tears. "You know," she said, "at first I thought you were so ugly. But now I see how beautiful you are. Thank you for saving my life – and my baby."

Frankenstein could only croak, "You're welcome," as he felt his heart radiate.

Goldie's recovery seemed to accelerate, with two exceptional milestones.

The first was the removal of her bandages. For this, her toughness was an asset.

"I used to be quite pretty," she said, "Let's see what I've done to myself."

First, the bandages were removed from her hands. They were red and blotchy and her fingers were just stubs. Goldie gasped and closed her eyes.

Then she opened them and said, "Looks like I'll be saving money on manicures. Let's keep going."

Her legs were similarly scarred and injured. Frankenstein felt as if his heart was being stabbed each time a bandage was removed.

Finally, it was time for her face and head. Mrs. Claus carefully removed the bandages from her tender skin and Goldie winced in pain. Frankenstein moaned when he saw the final results and Goldie joked with him through clenched teeth,

"You've got a lot of nerve, Scar Face. Hold up the mirror."

Frankenstein held up a hand mirror and saw Goldie's eyes take in her new hideous image. Tears squeezed out of her red-rimmed eye sockets. Small tufts of blondish hair dotted her damaged scalp and she reached a stubby hand up as though to smooth them. The look in her eyes changed from grief to a kind of acceptance and she quipped,

"As you can see, you must continue to call me Goldie."

The second milestone in Goldie's recovery was one of the most miraculous events ever to occur at the North Pole, and certainly in the life of Frankenstein. It was the birth of her baby.

She wanted Frankenstein to be there, and he became her birth partner. He coached her breathing, gave her ice cubes to suck on and encouraged her enthusiastically.

Mrs. Claus was a superb midwife who guided Frankenstein throughout the process. In the midst of this wonderful, terrifying, humbling, powerful event, Frankenstein wondered if this was what Victor Frankenstein had felt as he gave life to *his* creation.

When the baby emerged all pink and screaming, Frankenstein cut the umbilical cord and felt as proud and awestruck as any father has ever felt at the birth of his own child. He looked at the exhausted and happy Goldie and whispered in profound belief, "You are the most beautiful woman I have ever known."

The baby boy was perfect. Since Goldie had trouble holding him with her injured hands, Frankenstein helped her. Mrs. Claus took a photo of the three of them.

When the baby began to cry, Mrs. Claus arranged him in Frankenstein's arms and handed him a bottle. The tiny infant sucked eagerly at his first meal. His eyes were squinty and his little fists were held tight to his chest. Frankenstein marveled at the tiny perfect person.

"He's a good thing, isn't he?" Goldie asked. "I've done a good thing, haven't I?" She looked at her son with a mother's tired smile.

"Oh yes," said Frankenstein, "a very good thing."

She gazed at the pair, her face shining like an angel's. "I think I'll name him after my grandpa, the one good man in my previous life," she said, smiling at Frankenstein. "I think I'll call him Murray."

Despite her love for Murray, Goldie did not have much patience with him. She couldn't really hold him, so Mrs. Claus would prop her up with pillows, and then put Murray on her lap. One time, when Goldie tried to stroke Murray, her rough skin and clumsy moves caused him to jolt and let loose with a wail. Goldie yelled to Mrs. Claus, "Come get him! He hates me! I have no idea how to be a mother!"

"He's just being fussy, like any baby," said Mrs. Claus, scooping him up.

"Get him out of here!" Goldie barked and turned her head away.

Outside of Goldie's room, Mrs. Claus handed the teary-eyed Murray to Frankenstein, who held him to his chest and bounced him.

Mrs. Claus said, "We have to be understanding with Goldie. She has been through a lot and has a long way to go in her own healing – outside and inside."

Murray dozed off in Frankenstein's enormous arms.

"I understand," he said.

Over the course of a few weeks, Goldie continued to heal. She gained strength as well as tolerance for Murray. She held him in her lap more and watched his eyes follow her damaged hand, then grab it and giggle. She began to laugh too.

One evening, when Frankenstein came to see Goldie and Murray after work, he was stopped by a new beautiful sound coming from Goldie's room. He cracked the door open and saw Goldie sitting up with Murray on her lap. Frankenstein was shocked to see Gum strumming a guitar. Goldie, with her raspy voice, was simultaneously giving Gum instructions and then singing.

"Okay Gum – it's a G chord, then C, then G, D, E. Okay?"

Gum obeyed, and not badly, Frankenstein noted.

Goldie sang,

"Easy does it. This time is precious.

Don't let the moment go slipping away.

Keep your focus on ev'ry heartbeat.

Today is the moment for living today."

Frankenstein came all the way into the room and applauded. Gum stood tall and put the guitar behind his back, then relaxed and shrugged. Goldie grinned and said, "It's one of Grandpa's songs. He made it up. He would sing it when he brushed my hair. He used to call it *Murray's Song.*"

The baby cooed.

17. THE END, FOR NOW

Goldie grew stronger every day and the baby thrived. The elves enjoyed having a real human baby in the village and tested out their best infant rattles, musical mobiles and cuddly teddy bears on him. Murray was delighted with the attention and seemed to enjoy the tiny live creatures who chattered around him more than the toys they presented.

Goldie got fitted for prostheses, crafted by the finest wood carvers in the world. The doll makers fashioned a beautiful golden-haired wig for her and Taffy, the Elf Seamstress, made her some silky soft clothes with a new featherweight fabric she had designed so as not to irritate Goldie's sensitive skin. With tough determination, Goldie worked on her recovery.

Mrs. Claus got her walking and took her on tours of the village. Goldie admired the Toy Factory and all of the elf homes. She was most captivated by the greenhouses and chicken coops. She told Peeps, the Chief Elf Chicken Farmer, that she had worked a little with chickens on an urban farm in Seattle, and when she was feeling better she would like to help out with the farming.

"Like Frankenstein's maintenance work, this can be what I do!"

Peeps put her hands on her hips and said, "I could really use the help."

Despite her progress, despair would sometimes bubble up and Goldie would confess to Mrs. Claus, "I don't know how long I can keep this up."

"Can you do it for today?" Mrs. Claus would ask.

"Yes. I think so," Goldie would reply.

"Then one day at a time, dear, one day at a time."

Frankenstein blossomed in the role of "husband" and "father." He helped Goldie with her physical therapy and tended to Murray as often as Mrs. Claus and the elves would let him. He especially enjoyed the night feedings, which became his responsibility. It was then that he could have Murray all to himself and unhurriedly admire his perfect eyes, face and complexion. He adored watching the baby suck contentedly on a bottle while holding onto one of his enormous fingers.

During the day, Frankenstein went back to his work in the Toy Factory and all about the North Pole, preparing for his next Christmas trip. He was exhausted and energized all at once, like any new father, and found himself smiling and saying, "Danke, danke schön" out loud as he went about his many duties.

There was only a brief debate about whether Goldie and Murray would be permitted to stay at the North Pole. Gum argued that Goldie would eventually be missed and people would come looking for her. This could be a security risk. Goldie assured them that no one would miss her and Mrs. Claus stated the obvious.

"Who would think to look for her *here?*"

The matter was dropped.

The days, weeks and months flew contentedly by until it was once again the anniversary of Frankenstein's arrival at the North Pole.

Everyone gathered in the Great Hall to listen to Santa's Christmas speech. The three newest non-elf residents of the North Pole sat together: the hideous monster man, the scarred and crippled woman, and the tiny cooing baby.

When Santa spoke of the Holy Family, everyone stole a glance at the remarkable new "family" in their midst.

When he got to the part about the three Wise Men and their gifts, Santa paused – as he had never done in all the centuries of telling the story. He smiled and said,

"We of the North Pole are not accustomed to receiving presents. But we have been given three extraordinary gifts. Please join me in giving thanks for the beautiful gifts we have been given – the gifts of Goldie, Frankenstein and Murray!"

The cheering of elves made the air shimmer.

The End

Thanks to everyone who read drafts of *Frankenstein Meets Santa* and gave me comments. It was fun and fascinating discussing the Frankenstein and Santa tales with each of you . . . How big is Frankenstein compared to Santa and to the elves? Can you claim that Santa is "unconditionally loving?" What about the naughty kids and the whole he-sees-you-when-you're-sleeping thing? How can Frankenstein, who "lived" in the 19th Century appear at the North Pole in the year 2015? How *does* Santa get down and up a chimney, let alone Frankenstein? And, no, not every child gets a gift at Christmas.

Undoubtedly, the book is imperfect, but I tried to resolve most of the problems you pointed out. Thank you, first of all, to Julia Detering, my publisher and friend. Thanks to Ann Anderson Evans, Irene Hopkins, Katy Khadpour, Laura Lea King, Patty King Kuntz, Lance Lambert, Eileen Manger, Jan McCowan Box, Margaret Marquiss, John McDermott, Kirby McDermott, Patrick McDermott, Laura Musikanski, Constance Owen, Victoria Ries, Jo Simonian, Maggie Smith, Rumi Tsuchihashi and Andrea Zollo.

Thanks to my editor, Nancy Wick of Enlightened Edits, who gently pointed out things to fix, while offering her expert opinion and encouragement.

To Jan Harvey-Smith – how did you find the time to do your atmospheric drawings while working on the sets for the Pacific Northwest Ballet's newly designed production of *The Nutcracker*, and driving your twin girls to soccer? It's been an honor working with you.

To Jeanne Bellis, the amazing graphic artist who created the captivating cover – THANK YOU! I've known Jeanne since 5th grade – a long and meaningful friendship.

Last but not least, Frankenstein-sized THANKS to Laura Mueser, my friend and editor-psychologist-cheerleader, for reading various incarnations of this book and offering me the best and most helpful criticism, guidance and common sense.

For more information, go to: www.mjmcdermott.com
Or send an email to: info@mjmcdermott.com

When I asked Jim Harris, a clinical psychologist from Dallas, to read the book and perhaps write a "blurb" from the perspective of a psychologist, I was stunned to receive the following piece he offered. It was too long to use as a blurb, so I offer it here.

Frankenstein Meets Santa is so far-fetched a premise that one hesitates to even pick up the book, let alone read it. But not to read it would be a serious loss. Author M.J. McDermott marries an updated version of Santa Claus with the classic version of Frankenstein by wielding a psychological understanding of responses to suffering and the acting out of pain, eventually leading to redemption. The story is well paced, with a strong dialogue propelling a pro-family tale fit for both children and adults.

The pro-family underpinnings are bolstered with a nuanced and persuasive application of the two necessary ingredients for psychological well-being: the maternal and the paternal. Unconditional love in the form of caring for those unable to care for themselves without asking anything in return--the maternal. The redemptive virtues that arrive when one figures out how to make a contribution to the betterment of others, in the face of an indifferent world--the paternal. Of course, women and men have the capacity for both ways of being.

McDermott captures a true meaning of Christmas in a non-denominational manner, or even without regard as to whether one is a Christian: Jews, Muslims, Hindus, atheists, agnostics, etc. will identify with the universal human longing to be accepted and loved, and successfully wrestle with the evil monster inside (sin). We live on the learning planet, with suffering often driving the learning process. Each individual suffers in unique ways, but we all suffer. The source of the suffering may be from the vicissitudes of life, the happenstance of birth, or directly from the intentional/unintentional actions of others. What one does with their suffering matters. Is it directed destructively toward others? Is it possible to become aware of such and change? In Freudian terms, acting in accord with the ego ideal allows one to channel actions in a socially sanctioned manner leading one to happiness.

How is it possible to combine the most classic horror story of all time with a Christmas story and have the tale resonate psychologically and morally in compelling ways? Can Frankenstein find happiness? You must read this book and share it with your family to find out.

Jim Harris, Psy.D.
Clinical Psychologist
Dallas, TX
29-September-2015

Photo by Helen Nguyen

ABOUT THE AUTHOR & ILLUSTRATOR

Author M.J. McDermott is an Emmy Award winning broadcaster currently working as a meteorologist at Q13 FOX News This Morning, in Seattle, Washington. She has a degree in Drama from the University of Maryland and a degree in Atmospheric Sciences from the University of Washington. She lives in Seattle with her husband and twin sons. *Frankenstein Meets Santa* is her second novel.

Illustrator Jan Harvey-Smith has been drawing monsters since her childhood porch-sitting days in Pryor, Oklahoma. She has enjoyed the brief reliving of her doodling past with her creation of Frankenstein. As an artist, she has worked on both the east and west coast in the scenic art trade. She now resides in Seattle where she is the Master Scenic Artist at the Pacific Northwest Ballet.

Made in the USA
Charleston, SC
02 November 2015